{There Will Be No More Night}

THERE WILL BE NO
MORE NIGHT *{A Y2K Story}*

A Novel by Philip E. Sears

Overhill Press
MANHATTAN

Overhill Press

Published by Overhill Press
Manhattan, Kansas
OverhillPress@gmail.com

ISBN 979-8-218-33274-7 (paperback edition)
ISBN 979-8-218-33275-4 (ebook edition)

First Edition

Book design by Ashley Muehlbauer
Edited by Erica Smith

All quotations in chapter epigraphs
are from the public domain
and are credited to the authors.

Printed in the United States of America

{Prologue}

1/ EASTBOUND ON I-80

Spring 1999

NEBRASKA ... the good life
—Nebraska State Welcome Sign

Gordon barreled down I-80 eastbound through western Nebraska at eighty miles per hour in his '80s hatchback sports car. Wide open spaces, flat prairie land, corn fields, cattle, signs praising Jesus, for the next gas stop, nothing, fields, pastures, and more flat nothing. The occasional blessed general stores, where you can buy a slice of pizza or a wrinkled rotisserie hotdog, a soda, and fuel up with unleaded. Hurry to use the terrifying restroom, moldy green walls, toilet and sink stained black with waste and grease. An orange gallon pump of soap and a loose roll of paper towels. He would not risk washing his hands in that sink. Just don't touch anything.

The sunroof was open, hand on the gearshift, a cigarette between his fingers. The wind flapped loose papers in his back seat. His tobacco ashes swirled in the crosswind and then piled up in the hatchback among dead bleached-yellow insects. He was boxed in again by massive trailer trucks, their passing air waves shoving his car sideways like a toy. They were all grateful for I-80, a means to an end. This two-way exit through a sparse and mind-numbing prairie.

He was returning to his hometown of Lincoln, Nebraska's second city. And the great folks of Lincoln, Lincolnites, who lived in the capital city of a state with no real professional sports team, often referred, with misplaced pride, to the University of Nebraska's Memorial Stadium as the third largest city in the state. According to their foes' quips, The Big N of the Cornhuskers stood for Knowledge.

The University of Nebraska was Gordon's alma mater. Or, as he referred to it, his "almost matters"; he dropped out after his sophomore year to join the fast track. His tenure in business school made way to engineering; engineering segued into freelancing and "independent studies"; independent studies careened into a casual sit down with the assistant dean, a gentle bald man with ritualistic paddles on his office wall and a knack for talking to D students. And the rest, they say, is history.

He jammed out, singing off-pitch to a Third Eye Blind song. The treble was disrupted by the high frequency whipping of wind. The untrammeled bass thumped firmly on his lumbar. Yes, he did want something else. He wanted something else other than Nebraska and the farmland and friendly people.

On the highway, he recalled that youthful day, dreaming of his future. It was a high school summer day when he first got the quixotic notion that he would be somebody who changed the world. He wandered alone in his front yard, gallantly jousting with the large tree trunk. He was not going to grow up to be just another humble, hardworking Nebraskan. He was not going to be just some random nerd either. He had waves of visionary thoughts. He was going to be successful. But he was also going to have fun: a lot of fun. Work hard, play hard.

As he golfed a small rock at the old hickory tree, he focused inwardly on his dreams. The 1980s movies and shows that he watched longingly: Michael J. Fox in *The Secret of My Success,* where a Kansas State University graduate takes on New York City, working his way up in the corporate world. Gordon dreamed of walking downtown with a briefcase, passing by tall glass buildings—not looking up at them like a tourist—and commanding board rooms like he had seen on the silver screen. His hope was encouraged by famous Nebraskans before him: the Fonda Family, Henry who begot Peter and Jane. And Marlon Brando. Johnny Carson, King of *The Tonight Show*, who also graduated from the University of Nebraska in Lincoln. Warren Buffett, the Sage of Omaha, one of the richest men in the country.

There were others who shared his first name he felt he could look to. In some ways, he wanted to be like Gordie Howe, from Saskatchewan, the Nebraska of Canada, an ambidextrous and outstanding champion athlete. In other ways he looked up to Gordon Lightfoot, with his fame and creative talent for songwriting. Music: always providing a soundtrack for his life. Yet he was most inspired by the fictional Wall Street movie character Gordon Gekko. It was lost on him that Gekko was the villain. Instead, he found inspiration in his words: "Greed, for lack of a better word, is good." A million dollars liquid. Gordon recalled looking up *liquid* in an old dictionary, searching for a second meaning, other than water-like. An asset, Gordon learned, easily converted into cash. He had liked Gekko's expression, but that definition was not satisfying.

This was the source of his persona, and his imposter syndrome, as he learned in the future. Rarely he'd acknowledge this by saying he was just a "dumb shit from Nebraska," in the parlance of the Plains. From humble beginnings, it was a mountain for him to climb, but at the age of twenty-three, he was eager to summit.

Not all sweet business deals were made in Nebraska and Gordon felt on top of the world returning from a successful business trip to the West Coast. His team had visited San Francisco, where they had just met with some prospective business partners to explore a new opportunity. They stayed downtown, rode the cable cars, and took in a hilltop postcard view of Alcatraz in the bay. From the pier, the distant view of the Golden Gate Bridge, fragmented by fog. Surprised by the unexpected windchill in California, they had to purchase jackets, hopelessly trying to look more like savvy businessmen than tourists. At Fisherman's Wharf they walked down the pier and laughed at the barking sea lions. They met for a business lunch in Chinatown with Chastain. There was no ink to paper, but Gordon could feel in his gut that this was going to be a closer. ABC: Always Be Closing.

Gordon had driven through Tahoe National Forest, then to Nevada, cruising the seedy downtown casino district in Reno, and heading toward Utah on I-80. He took a scenic excursion to the southern region of Utah. A flatlander himself, he was always amazed to see snowcapped mountains. A remote beauty, Utah had been a pleasant surprise, rocks of every shade of brown and iron-rust red, forests, deserts, canyons, and crumbling buttes. He imagined himself an explorer of the Old West, a Spanish conquistador.

Back on I-80, he stopped at a desolate gas station, fueled up, pulled over into a dirt parking lot, and lit another cigarette. He folded out his road atlas on the top of the car in the sunlight, wiping the cigarette ashes off the wind-flapping page. He scanned the red, gray, and blue street lines that crowded around cities. He wandered the white spaces and green forests with black triangle peaks and lonely gray highways. After plotting the course, he calibrated his fingers on the mileage key in the Pacific Ocean, then measured the curvy road distances. Once on I-80, there were no more turns. The interstate went all the way home to Lincoln.

A drive across the country was just what he needed to get his head together. He had been burning the candle from both ends. Or more like a stick of dynamite with a short fuse. He had no idea how it had gotten that crazy. Success had a price. Higher than he had ever anticipated.

He needed to make a call to discuss a pressing matter but forgot his cellular phone charger. The incompatible adapter he purchased taunted him from the passenger seat. He found a phone booth on a main street in a bucolic Wyoming town. He dug loose change out of his sticky console.

"Hello?"

"Robert, it's me," Gordon said.

"Who is this?" Robert asked. "I don't recognize this number."

"It's Gordon, Robert. Don't be dense," Gordon said through the static.

"You sound weird. Where the hell are you?"

Robert had not been able to join the trip for some inexplicable reason, so Gordon wanted to catch him up on the events of the meeting. The meetup was successful, but Chastain had neglected any preparation, and Gordon had struggled to improvise without Robert's presence.

"Things are really heating up here. I can't talk about it. You need to get home," Robert said.

"I'm on my way. I'm feeling good about this new deal. Todd is right: Chastain is really making it rain. We missed you there, but I can't wait to catch you up," Gordon said, tearing off a filthy sticker from the plexiglass around the phone booth.

"I'm sorry, Gordon, but I have to go."

Gordon heard the dial tone. The heavy metal coil cable touched his forearm and a coldness crept through him.

{-----}

In Lincoln, Nebraska, Robert hung up the phone. He let out a pained sigh, leaning back on his sofa, palming his forehead, rubbing his clenched eyes.

An agent wearing a black jacket and vest walked into the room and stood over him.

"Robert, we need you to cooperate. You shouldn't have hung up like that; he was going to talk," the agent said.

"I *am* cooperating but I'm not going to bait him. I never agreed to that," Robert said, flustered.

The agent pressed his lips together, looked up and down, then picked up his clipboard and walked out of the room. The agent's partner emerged from the kitchen and followed him out.

Robert began to tear up. He did not know whether to cry, throw up, get angry or what. Mostly, he felt rage. He charged across the room and kicked a phone book.

"Goddamnit!" he shouted. He grated his teeth.

Robert's hound dog hunkered down and crept toward him, tail stiffly wrapped under her. She looked up at him, showing the whites of her puppy eyes.

"Oh, Betsie, I'm sorry, it's gonna be okay. Come here. Did you tinkle a bit, girl?"

Robert pulled from the roll of paper towels, giving it a bit of hell, spinning it around as he hastily tore off several squares. He wiped up the dog urine from the hardwood floor. He knelt tenderly, rubbing Betsie's ears to console her, gazing into her black-coal eyes.

2/ IN THE NEWS

Spring 1999

I have no proof that the sun is about to rise on the apocalyptic millennium of which chapter 20 of the Book of Revelation speaks, nor do I have proof that, armed with flood and catastrophe, the Four Horsemen will arrive on Jan. 1, 2000. Yet, it is becoming apparent to all of us that a once seemingly innocuous computer glitch relating to how computers recognize dates could wreak worldwide havoc.
—Senator Daniel Patrick Moynihan, D-N.Y.
Member, Senate Select Committee on the Year 2000 Technology Problem

Robert took off his shoes to kick back and unwind on the sofa. He patted the spot next to him. "Come here girl." Betsie jumped and curled up next to him and waited to be rubbed. Robert grabbed the remote control, trying not to disturb the dog. Betsie rested her head and sighed. Robert flipped through the cable channels.

"*. . . with three easy payments of $9.99 . . . But wait! That's not all! We'll throw in our patent pending mini hair crimpers, shower caps, professional salon quality hair combs, and an assortment of oils. All in your very own fashionable travel bag. All of this adds up to a true market value of $79.99. And we're throwing it all in for free!*"

Click.

"The country is in a panic about the Year 2000 computer glitch," the local news anchorman said. *"Experts are calling it the Y2K bug. Y2K is set to wreak havoc on power plants, banks, commerce, hospitals, and even the military. Does this Millennium glitch really spell doomsday or is it just a bunch of computer mumbo jumbo? Trisha sat down with our local computer expert, Dr. Schmidt, a Distinguished Professor of Computer Sciences at UNL, to get a better understanding."*

"No shit, Betsie. Remember Professor Schmidt?" Robert said.

Dr. Schmidt sat behind his desk in that familiar office, sporting a paisley necktie with a brown corduroy jacket and cream collared shirt. He had lost some hair but still wore the same glasses.

"So, could you try to explain that all again for our viewers, in less technical terms?"

"I'll do my best, Trisha. There are several different types of bugs that might be introduced by the year 2000 glitch. For instance, your bank may store your account information in a computer system called a database."

"A data . . . base? Is that a thing that holds all the information? Like a folder in a file cabinet?" Trisha asked. Robert wondered if she had been prepped with that analogy.

"Yes, Trisha, precisely. A database is the computer equivalent of a file cabinet that contains records. Instead of paper records, a database contains digital records. In fact, computer scientists also use the term 'file' for digital storage units. For example, a bank account stores your account information and transactions in digital records. In their database, they may have defined the year field in a database table as a two-digit field, rather than a four-digit field. So, for instance, a record with a year date of 1987 is stored as 87, and the year 1999 is simply stored as 99, and so forth."

"So, then the year 2000 is. Just, 00, zero?!" Trisha shook her feathered bangs and made her most startled panic face.

"Indeed. So, in this hypothetical example, on January 1st, 2000, the date would be set back erroneously to January 1st, 1900," the professor explained.

"So, I better take my money out of the bank then. Before they turn my balance into a big double zero too," Trisha said, turning her head to face directly into the camera.

"Well, I was just using that as an illustration. I can assure you that these problems will be resolved in time by professionals," Dr. Schmidt said. *"If they even exist."*

"*So, are you denying that there is a Y2K bug?*"

"*Of course not. I was invited here today to discuss the Y2K problem and explain issues by hypothetical example. We are merely speculating about where and whether these problems exist. Most of the known issues are trivial and will be resolved in time. The experts are no longer concerned about any major impact. Computer programmers and systems analysts have had plenty of time to—*"

Click. Click.

"Give me a break, Betsie," Robert said.

Click. *Static.* Click.

"*Be All You Can Be. Paid for By the US Army.*"

Click. *Laugh track.* Click.

"*Get all your local Lincoln news, sports, and weather at KLKN-TV. We'll be right back after a word from our sponsors.*"

Robert turned off the TV and tossed the remote onto the coffee table. He closed his eyes.

"Y2K!" His eyes flew open and he sprang up. He paced the carpet and grabbed fistfuls of his hair. Betsie stood on her short hind legs, pawing at him anxiously, falling off his sweeping legs. He strode back and forth across the living room. The memory struck him.

He rushed through the house and into the garage, grabbed a shovel, and flew out the back door. He headed into the backyard to a small, wooded area behind the shed. As he entered the brush and trees, he found a stone path hidden beneath bushes and branches. "One, two, three," he said, counting the spaced stepping stones. He wedged the shovel under the third stone, pulling it up and tossing it over. The newly exposed dirt was covered in a smooth, shiny membrane, crawling with worms and roly-polys. He dug deep, tossing clumps carelessly into the brush. At around three feet down his shovel hit hard metal. He dug around the hard object more carefully, dusting it off with his bare fingers. Finally, he pulled up a rusty old toolbox and crept it into the garage. Before examining his treasure, he peeked out the filthy cobwebbed window to see if anyone had been watching him. He set the toolbox on the garage floor. Betsie rejoined him to sniff the box around the edges.

"No, no, girl," Robert said. He pushed Betsie back and twisted open the box with a wrench. Inside were three giant orange medicine bottles. He shook one like a rattler. He hurried into his bathroom and spilled them into the toilet, flushing several times until nothing was left but discolored water. For some reason, Robert spared one last pill. He held it in his palm and inspected it closely. Just a small round item, chalky and textured, baby blue with sandy specks of brown and yellow. Pressed into the top of the cylinder-shaped pill were the letters *Y2K*.

"For old times' sake, right Betsie?" Robert tossed the pill into his mouth and swallowed it without water.

{Part 1}

3/ FIRST CLASS

Fall–Winter 1995

The best investment you can make, is an investment in yourself.
—Warren Buffett

In 1995, Tom Osborne would lead the Nebraska Cornhuskers through a perfect season and on to a second straight national championship. In Nebraska, that would just about qualify him for the governorship.

But Gordon was depressed that he was going to the University Nebraska–Lincoln in his hometown. UNL was a great value, but Gordon lacked school spirit. He would have preferred the old timer Bug Eaters mascot over a Cornhusker. *Anything not based on agriculture. And especially not a corncob wielding, straw-haired, redneck buffoon dressed in overalls and a red ten-gallon hat*, Gordon thought. He wished he was attending an Ivy league college like Dartmouth. He did not know where Dartmouth was located—probably the East Coast—or what their mascot was, though he was certain that it was not a farmer. He couldn't even pronounce Dartmouth. They would not have accepted him, and he could not have afforded it if they had. Dartmouth, for Rhodes Scholars and McArthur Genius fellows, was the Big Green. On the other hand, young Gordon, a Pell Grant recipient with a subsidized loan, matriculated at the Big Red.

Business was a natural choice if he was ever going to work on Wall Street and become a business titan like Gordon Gekko. He took some practical advice and minored in computer science. His math ACT score was high enough to get him into an engineering minor and Calculus I.

"It's the first day of class, don't sweat it," the young man at the next desk said. He wore a baseball cap, a goatee, and sideburns. "We'll probably just go over the syllabus and then he'll let us go."

Blackboards covered three walls. A heavy old wooden desk stood in front. Gordon took a deep breath and scanned the classroom of twenty or so male students.

He had dreamt of college. A charismatic professor sporting a tweed jacket theatrically addressing inspired students by name. Gordon's dreams were crushed, though, when the professor arrived. He was a disheveled middle-aged man in green sweatpants and tall white socks with colored stripes. He proceeded to kick off his sandals and get comfortable. For this seasoned, shoeless professor, sliding across the floor to markup calculations was plain sailing.

"What the fuck?" Gordon's goateed classmate exclaimed, just loud enough for him to hear.

The professor turned his back to the students and faced the blackboard and commenced intensely scrawling equations. He looked up and down from a small notepad like a bird feeding. After what seemed like ages, the professor turned to the class and looked out, wild-eyed, at his pupils.

"Calculate this derivative," he said with a thick accent that Gordon couldn't place. *That must be Eastern European. Maybe Yugoslavia, Czechoslovakia, or some Eastern Bloc country?*

There were the sounds of pages turning, pens scrawling, and the occasional whispers of collusion.

"Calculate this derivative," the professor said again, extending a piece of chalk.

A volunteer? Are you kidding me? No thanks.

Gordon's neighbor with the goatee stood up, his old metal chair screeching, and dashed to the front. To everyone's astonishment, he worked out the derivative. He returned to his desk and leaned back proudly. Gordon was awestruck.

The professor nodded and began furiously erasing with his right hand and scrawling equations with his left hand.

"Calculate *this* derivative!"

"Okay, cotangent . . . and then the *x* squared would be two *x*," the goateed student said, trying to workshop the problem out loud.

After a sweatpants-adjusting thinking-over, the professor solved the derivative. He punctuated the solution by breaking off the end of the chalk. He spun on his sock heels to face his perplexed pupils.

"Look here, the derivatives of the trigonometric functions," he said.

"But we haven't learned the cosecant function yet," a foolhardy student protested.

"The trigonometric functions, and the chain rule. That is not a Nebraska Law!" The instructor mocked the classroom with his thick accent. "This is not the Cornhusker rule!"

{-----}

Gordon was humbled by attending his hometown college, but he was not going to add insult by living with his parents. Consequently, he was placed in a dorm room in the northeast campus. His randomly assigned roommate was dark-haired, round, and chiseled out of dough. Gordon had never seen him leave the room.

"How was class?" Gordon asked. "What are you doing?"

"Playing *Doom*," his roommate said, pausing the game to take a big gulp from a thermos of soup. "No, I didn't go to class. Nothing ever happens the first week. They just hand out the syllabus. Or is it syllabi?"

"You're a freshman too, so how would you already know that?" Gordon watched as his roommate collected more armor. He paused the game and chugged more soup.

"I know things," his roommate said, returning to hammering on the keyboard, slaying pixeled Cacodemon with his shotgun. He turned up his battery powered PC speakers to drown out Gordon.

I'm not going to spend much time in this room. Not with him.

{-----}

Gordon spotted the same goateed student in his Computer Programming Languages class and sat nearby as they waited for the professor to begin.

"Hey, you following me? Just kidding. I'm Robert, by the way. Robert Schroeder."

"I'm Gordon. Gordon Hamilton. I'm a Lincolnite."

They shook hands.

"Computer science or computer engineering?" Robert asked.

"Neither. I'm a business major but I'm sort of minoring in computer science," Gordon said.

"Sort of? Who do you have for—"

"You may call me Dr. Schmidt or *Professor* Schmidt," the professor started. "Either is fine, or simply Professor. My primary duties are in research—rather than lecturing introductory courses—where I focus on real-time systems and embedded systems. We'll go over the syllabus and—"

A pale, bearded classmate interjected. "Pascal is a terrible language. Look at the clutter and unnecessary keywords. Anyhow, they should be teaching object-oriented languages, or something more elegant. If this old geezer kept up on modern coding languages, then we would be learning C++ rather than this obsolete procedural garbage."

"Turn to page seven in your text for the first course programming exercise written in an imperative language called Pascal—"

"Java will be the future of the world wide web," Robert said. "Have you heard of Java?"

"Keywords are reserved words that have a special meaning—"

"Java is too slow! It will never perform up against a language like C. Java code does not compile directly into native machine code like C. What about, uh, real time systems, or uh, what about, uh . . ." The impassioned student perspired through his Three Rules of Robotics T-shirt.

Gordon had never met young people who knew so much about computer programming.

"Anyway. Hey, we're sneaking some beers up to my dorm room Friday," Robert said under his breath. "You should come and join us. Harper Hall, Room 310."

"I like your style. I don't think I have anything going on then," Gordon said.

{-----}

In the evenings, Gordon cruised the old Havelock neighborhood imagining the glory days in the 1960s. Kids running through sprinklers, squealing with joy. Parents in driveways on aluminum webbed lawn chairs, sipping on cocktails and chain smoking, free to enjoy their groovy, freewheeling fun. The women sunbathing. The husbands dressed in dapper suits and fedora hats. Neighbors making rounds through the every-Friday block party. A father pushing up his aviator glasses, *"Hey Tom, can Ethel borrow a menthol?"* Tom, pulling out a soft pack from his dress shirt pocket, winking. *"Sure, pal, anything."*

Gordon's childhood summers in the 1980s were like suburban kids in a Stephen King novel or a Steven Spielberg movie. Children free-ranged all day until sunset signaled curfew. Parents shouting names from front porches. They could not even fathom a need for the internet. They desired nothing more advanced than arcade video games with one screen worlds. Urban myths could propagate uncontested before the age of the truth machines. *"What did Richard Gere do?"* Cory B asks. And Cory C answers, *"Who cares, last one to the stop sign is a rotten egg."* And then race BMX bikes down the block, swinging handlebars left and right to build momentum.

When Gordon was young, he rode his bike through these same Havelock streets. He made many passes by a modest brick house with a side garage. Gordon found something extraordinary about the little blond girl named Tonya. Sometimes, if he saw Tonya home, he would pop wheelies or jump the curb. She was often out playing or drawing on the driveway with colored chalk. She did not seem to notice him.

Tonya was a year younger. That would make her a senior in high school. Gordon wondered if she still lived there. He didn't see her on that evening drive. So, he turned up his music and drove back home.

Gordon arrived in the dorm room after the liquor had made the dangerous journey up the fire escape of the "dry" dorm hall. Robert's roommate Michael shoved the new R.E.M. album *Monster* in his CD player. Michael Stipe crooned "Star 69" over edgy new guitar effects. Robert leaned against the top bunk, talking to a young man tucked in the shadows of the lower bunk.

"I didn't think you'd show up," Robert said, greeting Gordon with a sliding palm handshake. "Hey, this is Oliver."

Gordon nodded to Oliver. Oliver anxiously shook his chubby cheeked face several times, mouthing a few inaudible words.

Robert continued, ". . . but we call him Frodo."

"Why?" Gordon asked, giving Oliver only a cursory glance.

"Cause he's from the Land of Hobbits," a new voice answered from behind Gordon.

"This is Todd Wallace," Robert said as Gordon turned. "He lives on this floor. Sophomore, studies Computer Science too."

"And it's Middle-earth," Oliver said, scowling timidly.

Todd was a young man around nineteen years old, with short, gelled, frost-tipped hair, and a hemp necklace. He wore a white tank top, commonly called a wifebeater, exposing a black, orange, and yellow sun tattoo on his left shoulder. Silver earrings pierced both his ears and his jeans were just the right amount of loose fitting, not skateboarder baggy, but still fashionably cool. He had smooth, unblemished skin and a well-proportioned face suitable for a boy band. He leaned on the bunk bed, his armpit hair on full display. Gordon smelled his pungent cologne.

"So, Frodo, how'd that date go last night?" Todd said. Gordon found his dimpled smile unkind.

"What are you talking about, Todd. I didn't have any date." Gordon noticed a slight speech impediment and a childish inflection in Oliver's voice, where r's turned to w's. Oliver leaned back into the shadows. Gordon watched him pull on his t-shirt, stretched tight over his belly rolls.

"Why don't you talk to some of the girls down the hall? They're probably more afraid of you than you are of them. Like the wild animals on PBS documentaries." Todd laughed at his own joke. He turned to Gordon. "How about you, dude? Do you have a girlfriend? Or did you at least invite some ladies to the party tonight?"

"No, I don't have a girlfriend. Well, it's sort of just . . . I just think it's better to be good on my own first. Anyway, I don't want to deal with all of that," Gordon explained.

"Oh, I hear ya, bro. Did your high school sweetheart break your heart or something?" Todd grinned obnoxiously.

"Kind of, not really," Gordon said. "But dating is just a bunch of trouble I don't want to deal with. I've been through a few things and now I'm trying to figure myself out."

"A wise man once said, *Owner of a lonely heart, much better than an owner of a broken heart*," Robert's roommate Michael said.

"That's right. Respect." Todd looked for unnecessary handshakes but was left hanging. "Hey, bro," he said to Robert, "I'm about due for another one of those Mickey's." Robert handed Todd and Oliver another green grenade-shaped bottle of malt liquor.

Gordon noticed that Oliver was sweating and pulling on his t-shirt again. He saw the look of revulsion that crossed Oliver's face as he brought the bottle to his mouth. He looked like he was trying to choke down cough syrup as his eyes watered.

They were lucky to have a visit from two females looking lost in the hallway. The first coed, a sophomore, had dark shoulder length hair, round glasses, and an athletic build. Her friend in tow, a freshman, was petite with long straight, dishwater blond hair. They entered the room and introduced themselves as Jennifer and Becky. Michael, the aspiring DJ, flipped through the music for something appropriate for the new mood. Todd stretched his arm out casually across the bunk, trying to lean like James Dean.

"Would you two like something to drink?" Robert asked.

"Sure," Jennifer said. "What do you have?"

"We have beer, schnapps, everything." Robert beamed.

"Do you have any Zima or Boone's? Or, like cider?"

"I don't think so, come look. Help yourself."

Jennifer approached the boxes of alcohol on the other side of the room, leaving Becky to fend for herself.

Gordon listened to Robert talk to Jennifer. He might have even heard cheerful rapport. *What is going on, are they already laughing and having fun?* Oliver had still not left his post on the lower bunk, increasing his t-shirt pulling cadence. His face was flushed and splotchy.

"What are you majoring in?" Becky asked Gordon.

"Business," Gordon answered, and he felt the blood rush from his head to his hands, where it was least needed.

"You're not an engineer? I thought this was an engineering student party," Becky said.

"Yes, it is, but not exclusively. I think I'm the only non-engineer, but I'm minoring in computer science too. That's how I know Robert, from programming . . . and math class. So, what do you major in?"

Come on Gordon, you're not supposed to ask that question.

"Mechanical engineering," Becky said. "Sorry, I'm sorry. I forgot to say that."

"It's no biggie."

"Does that surprise you?"

"Does what surprise me?"

"That a little blond girl is studying mechanical engineering?"

"No," Gordon said. "I didn't say that. It's just . . . mechanical engineers are typically farm boys from the country, right?"

No answer.

He needed to change the subject. "So, you know Robert then? For how long, for, uh how did—?"

"Yes, I know Robert and Michael. But I met them last week at the mixer. I'm a freshman so everyone is new here."

"Oh, me too," Gordon said. Amazing discovery, they had something in common.

Robert, Jennifer, and Michael carried on with chatting and laughter, an afront to Gordon's awkward exchange with Becky. *Those carefree fools.*

"Well, I know Jennifer. We went to Westside High School together in Omaha," Becky said.

Becky held her hands together and twisted one of her feet. Silence was golden. Not precious and rare, but heavy, dense, and difficult to break down.

"So, do you want something to drink?" Gordon finally asked.

"I don't think . . . well, okay, yeah," Becky said.

As soon as they converged on one circle of conversation, Gordon no longer had to play one-on-one defense. Todd passed around drinks for everyone.

{-----}

It was not long after that fateful dorm visit that Jennifer and Robert started dating, on and off again. And on again. Jennifer tried and failed, over and over, for Gordon to double date with them. But Gordon resisted being set up with Becky, or anyone for that matter. There was only Tonya. But, like beachfront property in Arizona, there was no real prospect.

Throughout the fall semester, the boys served out the compulsory week-days, going through the motions of early alarm clocks, straining not to fall asleep during class, eager to get to the weekend. Gordon wanted to run out the clock on college. *How will I ever get through three more years of lectures and homework? I just want to make it out of here; work hard, play harder.*

They established a private backwoods spot called the Range for all-night party sessions. The smell of freedom: dewy air, cheap domestic beer, and campfire smoke. Coolers packed with ice cold beer cans. The smoke clinging to their clothes and hair for days. Oliver busying himself, gathering branches for firewood, talking to himself in a delightful stupor, the loud chirping of insects obscuring the distant fireside chatter.

They frequented the Range not only for drinking and freedom but to philosophize. They idolized writers like Henry Miller, Charles Bukowski, and Jack Kerouac, who romanticized a life of liberation. They wanted to be like beatniks or hippies. But they were products of the materialistic '80s Reagan-era money for nothing MTV vanity pop culture. Yet they still yearned for their own idealistic counterculture movement.

4/ AG TECH

Spring 1996

Surround yourself by people who take their work seriously, but not themselves, those who work hard and play hard.

—Colin Powell

In the spring, Robert joined the Omaha-based agricultural technology company FarmTrepid and made a great first impression. And since FarmTrepid was looking for some more affordable summer help on their web team, Robert referred Gordon and landed him a part-time web programmer job.

Gordon had his first sit-down with the manager, O'Neill. O'Neill was a gentle, middle-aged man with a soft, lightly freckled complexion and a trimmed golden beard with reddish hair. "A real *salt of the earth* guy," Robert had said. "He's a church-going man who teaches Sunday school to junior high school students, but so far as managers go, he's jovial and easygoing."

"What are you studying at UNL?" O'Neill asked Gordon, leaning back casually, resting his hands on top of his belly.

"Business. But I'm also minoring in computer science," Gordon said.

"Business? Ha, what kind of business? Just business, eh? I hope you're not planning on being poor," O'Neill said, shaking with silent laughter.

"I'd really like to start my own business too. Someday soon." Gordon offered this goal unsolicited. "So, this would help me gain some experience."

"Okay, well, that sounds good. Anyway, let me show you were we gotcha set up." Gordon followed O'Neill to his new office space.

{-----}

A drab rectangle room enclosed a cubicle farm in a plain rectangle strip mall on a rectangle city block. Each cubicle held a color monitor with a thirteen-inch screen the weight of an American child, powered by a tower PC which also functioned as a space heater. Robert and Gordon shared neighboring cubicles. Robert often rolled his chair back to get Gordon's attention, as Gordon typically listened to music while immersed in programming HTML pages for the company website.

Proud of his own office space, Gordon pinned a poster of Jack Parsons on his cubicle wall. Jack Parsons looked dapper in his suit and tie, wavy black hair, and Howard Hughes mustache. Parsons was Gordon's *work hard, play hard* poster boy: a rocket scientist, Caltech associate, founder of NASA's Jet Propulsion Laboratory, and a key player in the inception of the US space program. In his free time, Parsons was a philosopher, occultist, writer, drug user, and host of ritualistic drug-fueled orgies.

One day O'Neill strolled by Gordon's cube and asked, "Now, who is that gentleman?"

Gordon answered, "Jack Parsons, inventor, rocket scientist."

But Gordon imagined saying to his God-fearing boss, *Pagan occultist who tried to create a spawn of Satan. Worshipper of Pan. Host of drug-fueled sex rituals at his Pasadena lodge. Shared a teenage lover with L. Ron Hubbard, founder of Scientology. A frequent correspondent with satanic magician Aleister Crowley, known as the Wickedest Man in the World, and so on.*

Gordon clicked the Windows 95 Start Menu, expanded it, and opened his favorite text editor app, used for web programming. He was currently developing a screen for company announcements. After completing some HTML programming, he was ready to test his new <BLINK> tag </BLINK> for this webpage. He saved the file changes and tested it locally in his Netscape 2.0 browser. And Gordon said, *Let there be tiled background with a scanned Nebraska farm image.* He saw text blink over tiled background and knew that it was good.

He watched the blink tag in action from his browser, flashing an important example announcement. He was deeply satisfied.

"Did you hear me?! I've been talking to you for several minutes," Robert exclaimed.

"What?!" Gordon asked, pulling off his headphones.

"About news from the markets. You know, the weather report. And soybean futures. Also, did you hear about—"

"Oh, give me a break." Gordon turned away and reached for his headset.

"Hey, what's your hang up, Gordon? I don't understand," Robert said.

"What do you mean?"

"You have this problem with agriculture. We work at an ag tech company. You do, Gordon. I don't get it."

"Why should I care about corn fields and soybeans? Don't you want something different in life? Something besides barns and windmills? Can't we rise above and beyond? And be more cultured?" Gordon asked.

"You're from Nebraska, too. Gordo, you're just like the rest of us. Everyone from around here has ancestors that moved from back east or from Europe to settle and farm," Robert said.

"I don't," their co-worker Vikram Singh chimed in. Robert ignored him.

"Can't you be proud?" Robert jumped up from his chair, a fervent look in his eyes. Gordon put his headset back down on his desk and stood, too.

"Be proud of farming?" he asked. "Why? Does everyone need to be proud? Are the Soviets proud of their Motherland? Of their totalitarian communist state?" He was aware his voice was rising with each word, so that when he finished his final sentence he was practically shouting in Robert's face. "Would you be a proud Soviet, Robert? Huh, comrade?"

The USSR non sequitur broke the tension.

"Hahaha." Robert laughed and patted Gordon jovially.

"Actually," Vikram said, "agriculture itself was the seed for civilizations to flourish, providing an abundance of food, allowing many citizens time to take up different occupations."

Robert nodded approvingly. "That's right, Vik. Without agriculture and farming, Gordon, we would not be able to pursue our specialized professions. Like art, politics, engineering . . . Or programming websites."

Gordon would not argue along those lines. He was trying to come up with something else to stump them. *Farming should no longer interest young people. Not in the '90s.*

Another co-worker, Stuart, sauntered over to the huddle. He donned his walker hat, Gordon thought, to appear wise beyond his nineteen years.

"Many new studies now put into question whether urban civilization benefits the greater good of the majority, or just an elite minority," Stuart began professorially. "Civilization has undeniably led to technological innovation and wealth for a privileged minority. Having said that, most advanced civilizations were built on the backs of slaves, serfs, or a poor working class."

"But what about the poor primitive country folks," Gordon said, "that would not have the advances in technology and medicine offered by cities? In fact, I learned in business school that in China, rural people are happy to move to the cities and away from the farms, even without skilled, high-paying jobs. Younger people, especially young Chinese women, are leaving the countryside villages for cities to seek out freedom and opportunity."

Vikram laughed and asked incredulously, "Have you ever *been* to Asia? Or even left the United States?"

Vikram did not conform to the style of baggy pleated khakis and faded knock-off polos and instead wore a well-groomed beard, an indigo blue turban, new pressed black denim jeans, a button-up collared shirt tucked in, a tan leather belt, and brown leather dress shoes. He was arguably the most stylish man in the office.

Gordon and Robert had never seen Vikram get angry or display any hatred toward anyone. Vikram was truly a proud American citizen who loved *The Simpson's*, the NFL, bourbon whiskey, and the band 311, who happened to hail from Omaha. Vikram had detailed to them, numerous times, what a typical interaction was like when he was introduced to a Nebraska native:

"So, where are you from?" the Nebraskan would invariably ask.

"I'm from Omaha," Vik would answer.

"No, I mean, where are you *from*? I mean, *originally*," the dissatisfied Nebraskan would press on.

"I'm from Omaha, Nebraska. I graduated from Westside High School. My family moved from California when I was very young." Vikram would explain patiently.

The Omaha finance industry, not farming, brought Vikram's family to Nebraska.

"Life expectancy in the great western cities, like New York, LA, London, is lower than their rural countryside counterparts," Vikram said.

"That is not saying much," Robert said. "Come on boys let's get back to work."

They returned to their cubicles. Gordon knew the discussion was one they could have forever and not come to a consensus on.

{-----}

Windows tabs multiplied like dominos across Stuart's taskbar. He panicked as he tried to close them and clicked cancel, causing tabs to spawn even more and more tabs.

"Mission accomplished," Robert said, laughing. They were all laughing like schoolgirls. Vikram smiled uncomfortably.

"We're only messing with Stuart. He's such a spaz. He's not even asking for our help," Robert said.

Stuart pulled his jacket off the rack, put on his hat, and stormed out of the office. They froze in silence.

Stuart had been the target of many pranks but never ceased calling attention to himself. He habitually mentioned his aspirations to become a volcanologist. He posted a scientific volcano diagram on his cubicle walls identifying everything from the magma chamber to the eruption cloud and acid rain. He also brought in some of his own furnishings, including a wooden hat rack. All of this made him popular at work.

"All right, girls. Fun is over," O'Neill said, walking down the hall by the cubicles. "It's time for the weekly status meeting."

5/ SOWING THE SEEDS

Summer 1996

To take all you want
Is never as good.
As to stop when you should.

—Lao Tzu, 4th Century BC

Robert and four other friends rented an old house when they were able to move out of the dorms. The backyard faced an alleyway with parking such that it was hard to tell where the lawn ended and the parking started. Underneath the canopy of trees, they dug a semi-permanent bonfire where they planned to burn leaves, branches, and trash until reported to the authorities. And so their Wednesday Night Sessions began.

It was at the weekly outdoor hangout that Gordon first encountered Damian Charlock. Damian seemed strange to Gordon on first impression, with his baggy clothes and skater haircut, not to mention his clear obsession with chemistry woven into many conversations.

"What are you going to do when you graduate?" Robert was asking. He glanced up when Gordon came over and sat down next to them around the bonfire. "Gordon, this is Damian Charlock. Damian, this is my good friend, Gordon."

"Hey, man, what's up," Damian said, extending his hand so he and Gordon could slap palms.

"Not much," Gordon said.

"Gordon, you have big plans, right?" Robert asked.

"I'm already tired of school. I just want to get into business as soon as possible and start making some money. I'm not sure why we have to take so many of these elective classes. Chemistry, biology, geology."

"I know what you mean. I hate chemistry," Jennifer said.

"Chemistry class is boring. Chemistry in action is beautiful," Damian said. "If I graduate in chemistry, I'm probably going to end up doing lab work. But I've always wanted to have my own lab."

"I switched from a business major with a computer science minor to just computer science," Gordon said. "It was too much. I figure technology is where the money is at. But do you really need all that extra coursework to get into the profession? Let's get on with it."

"Yeah. Forget all that school. You all should start your own business. You and Robert," Damian said.

"Yes, that's what I'm talking about. But, doing what? And who with?"

Damian considered this. "You should start your own software company."

"Yeah," Robert said, "let's launch a software startup."

"That's a good idea, but with who, doing what?" Gordon asked.

Robert grinned. "Gordon, you should be our CEO!"

"President and CEO, Gordon Hamilton," Jennifer said. "Sounds presidential, anyway."

"Yeah, Gordon, you're the visionary," Oliver said. "This has always been your dream. You have the vision."

"Do I?" Gordon asked, wading in a confluence of self-doubt and egotism. *I'm a dreamer, all right. But do I have vision and leadership?*

"Sure, you do. You're the natural—well, dreamer, Gordon," Jennifer said.

"But we'd need money to start a company."

"You can find investors. People do this all the time," Jennifer said.

"Yeah, people do. But what about Nebraska students sitting outside burning trash and getting high?"

"Okay, but these founders of startups . . . don't they typically have friends and family as investors?" Robert asked.

"That's true," Jennifer said. "Not everyone has the same opportunity.

Most successful software entrepreneurs had money or were in the right place at the right time. Bill Gates, Steve Jobs, all the—"

"I know Bill Gates was privileged, Jenny, but are you sure about Steve Jobs? I thought he was from a broken family?" Robert said.

"Well, he wasn't as well-off as Bill Gates, but he was still raised in Palo Alto, California. That's like Silicon Valley, isn't it?"

"Imagine if he would have grown up in rural Nebraska, like Oliver," Gordon mused. "I doubt he would have met Steve Wozniak harvesting corn or working at a hardware store."

"Yeah, he'd be like my papa wearing overalls. Papa doesn't even know how to turn on a computer," Oliver said.

"Who do we know that knows someone with money?" Robert asked.

Gordon frowned, thinking. "Doesn't Todd Wallace come from money? Maybe he has some connections. He talks a big game, doesn't he?"

"Yeah, he talks big," Jennifer said. "Where is he, anyways? I haven't seen him around for a while."

"He's out with his new friends," Robert said. "They follow some glam rock or new wave band. They're pretty into it. Into themselves, anyway."

Robert looked at Damian. "Aren't you into the music scene around here?"

"Yes, but not those bands. I'm into jam bands like Phish, and the rave scene. The rave scene is finally coming to Nebraska."

Damian handed Gordon a flyer from an Omaha rave. Gordon was enticed by the entrancing graphics and simple info about the DJs and venue. His imagination ran wild with the imagery. And the mystery of what was not written on the flyer.

"Can I keep this flyer?" he asked.

"It's yours. Even better: Let's go together," Damian said.

Silence fell over the group. The fire crackled and popped. The skunky marijuana smoke mingled with the fast-food trash and woodfire.

"I can ask Todd after he gets home from the show," Robert said.

"About what?" Jennifer asked.

"About if he's connected. If he has money, for the startup."

"Right. That," Jennifer said. Gordon looked at her, trying to tell if she was intentionally being patronizing. "But what software are you making? What have you guys made? Why would anyone want to invest in you?"

"We'll still need some time to figure out all those details," Gordon said.

Jennifer regarded him and then got up and left without saying anything. A moment later, Robert got up and followed her.

"Where are they going all of the sudden?" Oliver asked.

Damian shrugged and exhaled a curling plume of smoke. The fire crackled. Gordon stared into the dancing flames as Damian coughed. Something was telling him to go check in on Robert.

He went upstairs to the bathroom and afterward, passed by Robert's room. Robert was hunched over on his bed.

"I was wondering where you went," Gordon said from the doorway. He slowly stepped into the room.

Robert stared across the room and didn't respond. Gordon couldn't tell if he was angry or sad or what.

"What's wrong? You can tell me," Gordon said. He turned a desk chair around, pulled it next to the bed, and sat down.

Robert's eyes reddened. He looked away from Gordon, and addressed the wall as he fought back tears. "Jennifer isn't sure if she wants to be with me. I feel like she doesn't love me anymore. Or maybe there's someone else."

"You guys seemed okay tonight. Well, she did sound a little skeptical that we would ever have something someone would want to invest in. But otherwise—You were both just being your typical friendly selves out there by the fire."

"It's just an act. She won't even talk to me when we're alone. It's torture."

"I know how it feels, Robert. It's like one day you are holding on to her closely. Then the next day you see her next to you but like she's a million miles away."

The dam broke and tears rolled down Robert's cheeks.

Gordon put his left hand on Robert's right hand and clenched it.

"I'm sorry, Robert. I know how it feels. Just give it some time. Talk to her, maybe."

"Do you think there's someone else?"

"No, of course not. Stop imagining things," Gordon said sternly.

Robert swung his feet over the bed and sat up like he was ready to face the music. He wiped his eyes and stretched his back.

"How about a round of drinks? Maybe something strong," Gordon suggested. "Or do you want a glass of warm milk before bed?"

"Sure, Gordo, I'll go with something strong," Robert said.

"How about some Southern Comfort?"

"Oh, God, no! I'll get sick if I even smell that stuff again," Robert said, cheering up.

Gordon patted Robert on the shoulder firmly and headed to procure libations.

"*Aaaaaaaaahhhhh!*" There was a bloodcurdling scream from downstairs, followed by loud stomping and swinging doors.

"The hell was that?" Robert asked.

"You stay right here. I'll go see what happened," Gordon said, striding out of the room and down the stairs, where he met Jennifer in the hallway outside the bathroom.

"I was in the bathroom when something tickled my leg," she said breathlessly, "and I saw this furry thing slide under the door. It was bigger than a rat and had a furry tail, so, like, I didn't know what it was. What the hell was it?"

Gordon smiled. "That's just Reginald, Oliver's ferret. He's harmless. Must've gotten out of his room. Nothing to freak out about."

"That thing scared me!" Jennifer exclaimed. "I love furry critters. I just didn't know what it was." She shook her head, clearly embarrassed as everyone from outside gathered in the hallway to see what the commotion was.

"Just think of him as a stinky slinky," Gordon said.

"Stinky slinky? Oh, that's funny, I like that."

"What happened to Reginald?" Oliver asked. "Is he okay? Where is he? I hope nothing bad just happened to him!"

"Everything's fine," Gordon said.

The crowd disbanded. Gordon snagged a bottle and headed back to Robert's room. He passed Oliver in the dark upstairs hallway holding Reginald in his arms, stroking him.

"Let's get you back in your room," Oliver was saying. Gordon stopped and turned, overtaken by curiosity. He followed closely behind Oliver.

Gordon experienced culture shock upon entering Oliver's room. There was barely any human furniture. The floor was covered by lime green shag carpet, giving the effect of entering a meadow. The bed was simply a mattress in the far corner with a bare pillow, sheets, and a blanket. A digital alarm clock rested on the carpet next to the mattress, a black cord snaking its way through the shag carpet. A heap of clothes was piled on the floor, and another spilled out of a small doorless closet. Opposite the mattress was a large contraption of wooden shelving, orange tubes, and ramps, assembled with erector sets and other items like some hillbilly Rube Goldberg device.

Gordon knew that this was for the ferret. And judging by the masking tape, it was homemade. Oliver released Reginald into the hill of clothes. The ferret bounced off the laundry pile, slunk across the room, weaved up the shelves in the contraption, and flew through several tubes with astonishing speed.

Gordon backed away before he was noticed. Robert had turned on his black lights and lava lamp and arranged a couple bean bags for them to sit on.

They spent the rest of the night sipping rum and throwing darts at the wall across from the beanbag chairs. Robert thanked Gordon for his friendship.

"I'm feeling much better," Robert said.

6/ RAVE REVIEW

Fall 1996

... dancing in the same room and the same dance to the same music,
and whose radiant faces floated past me like fantastic flowers,
belonged to me, and I to them. All of us had a part in one and other.

—Hermann Hesse, *Steppenwolf*

The hatchback barreled toward Omaha on a dark highway carrying the party of four. Gordon sat with Damian in the front while Damian's girlfriend Debbie and Robert were in the back. Gordon stared out at the bleak and colorless midwinter prairie.

"Hells yeah. Looks like some bangin' beats tonight," Damian said. "We've got drum and bass from Brooklyn, techno DJ from Detroit, and some local hard house DJs."

"Let's hear some of the rave music, then!" Robert said.

Damian shoved a CD into the stereo and electronic drumbeats blared from the side speakers, accompanied by deep bass lines. Gordon found it jarring, almost terrifying and hostile. It seemed to have no rhyme or reason. Damian nodded his head to the beat and shifted his hand in the air like automatons.

"That was a drum and bass mix from a New York DJ. I didn't have any mixes of this DJ from the Bronx, but I bet he'll be spinning these kinda d n' b records, probably older stuff," Damian explained.

"Do you have any of the local music?" Gordon asked.

"Oh yeah, I do. This is some straight up house music." Damian changed CDs. The four on the flour beat and disco-funk bass lines felt more familiar and Gordon was able to find his groove. He pondered the prosaic genre name of "house music" and imagined a DJ playing at a house party.

They found their destination in an industrial park on the outskirts of Omaha. The building was not a bar or club; it was not identified by any signage. Although the building looked sprawling and vacated, cars had filled the parking lot. They drove around to the side and parked in the dusty grass. *Now this is the underground scene.*

They joined the long line of people waiting to get through the front door security. It was a chilly night, yet the partygoers were warm with anticipation, puffing clouds of mist in clear view of the flood lights. These party people looked like a Dr. Seuss book come alive. Bright primary colors, large plush hats, neon wigs, spiked hair, tight bright shirts, wide leg jeans the width of dresses, beads and candy necklaces, whistles, pacifiers, blinky lights and glowsticks, fit young men wearing angel wings, girls with tight halter tops, navels exposed to the cold, and baggy camo pants. Gordon became self-conscious of his style, plainly dressed in a collared shirt and straight fitted jeans.

A young man in a hoodie walked up and down the line asking, "Anyone want some Special K? Breakfast of champions. Anyone miss their breakfast? K?"

"What's that?" Robert asked. "You're our resident expert."

"Special K, ketamine. It's a dissociate," Damian said.

"Horse tranquilizer," Debbie said to Gordon. She wore a white bandana over her blue ponytails and was adorned with a wide array of bracelets and necklaces.

"Don't worry, it's not what you want. Not for now," Damian said.

"Should we be asking for E then? Or some drinks or something?" Gordon asked.

"No, you don't need to do that here. Be patient, dude," Damian said, "Let me tell you bro. It's all about people and music and exploration of the mind. Only on weekends and events like raves. Never by yourself. That is our psychonaut raver philosophy. Always in the right atmosphere with good vibes and great people. Must have good music. It's about the music and the people before drugs."

They paid the cover and were granted entrance. The main room was dark and smoky, except for the strobe lights flashing from the stage and light coming in from the far entrance. The walls had been tagged with glowing graffiti and makeshift murals. People had begun crowding at the opposite end where a DJ was spinning records from the front stage.

They encountered hardcore dancing and intense music as they pushed toward the stage. A baggy jeans raver was spinning lights on strings in S-shaped patterns like a Polynesian island ceremony. *The party people are dancing together but not like the clubs that I've gone to in the city. The men aren't trying to grind on the women or pick up on them. They are deep in the music.*

Debbie, clearly a free spirit, had already fallen into a drum circle of tie-dyed hippies with accompanying bongos. They met a brother and sister from Omaha who both wore their dishwater blond hair in long dreadlocks. Robert asked if he could feel the sister's hair but was denied with prejudice. Damian closed his eyes and grooved to the music. Robert nudged Gordon and they stood up to join a different circle that had formed to watch breakdancing b-boys. The b-boys dueled with popping and locking, floor spins, and deft one-handed air freezes.

Later, Robert signaled toward a couple side rooms where they could hang out away from the dance floor. In the first room—which originally served as a large break room—they realized that people were already making themselves extremely comfortable, lying down on mats and being rubbed down by each other. One raver sprawled on his back, shirtless and sweaty, mouth and eyes clenched. Then another man put something white in his mouth and straddled over him to blow something in his eyes. A girl wearing a visor and baggy pants leaned against the wall while her friend held her arms and stroked them slowly. The steadily thumping bass was more felt than heard. Gordon glanced over at Robert, who looked confused or maybe even shocked. They had both certainly sobered up quickly.

Damian led them from the room, pulled them aside to the main room away from the speakers.

"Crazy stuff, huh. Robert, you look like you've seen a ghost," Damian said.

"I don't even know *what* that was. I would know a ghost if I saw one," Robert said.

"You guys ready to party? I'm sure we can find a hookup. Gordon, do you want to ask around? Just don't ask for *ecstasy* like you've never been here. Just say, 'Do you have any rolls?'"

"Rolls?"

"Yes, rolls. They call it rolling here," Damian said.

"That's strange, I wonder why," Robert said.

"Debbie, do you want anything, baby?" Damian asked.

"Not tonight," Debbie said. "I'm already having fun. Besides, I may need to babysit our new travelers."

They lit cigarettes and stood silently in their huddle.

"Well, here goes nothing," Gordon said.

He walked toward the heaving crowd, around the breakdance circle, and closer to the front stage. Gordon looked at people that might have potential but could not muster the nerve to ask. Finally, he approached a savvy raver with baggy jeans and a pacifier.

"You got any rolls?" Gordon asked.

"What's that?" The raver stopped dancing to listen politely.

"You have any rolls?" Gordon repeated.

"Oh, it's too early in the evening to be asking for that," the raver answered, and then began dancing again. Gordon was discouraged but at least he had broken the ice. *It's past eleven. Not exactly early. And everyone here is complicit. No Nancy Reagan Say No club members here.*

"Wassup, man, I'm looking for some party favors. You got any rolls?" Gordon asked another random raver.

"Oh, yeah, I can probably hook you up, dude," the raver said. He leaned toward Gordon's right ear. "How many do you need?"

"I want three. I have two friends with me."

"Whatever's clever. They're twenty-five. You got the bills?"

Gordon looked in his dark pocket where he had folded some twenty-dollar bills. He counted out four and handed them over.

"There's eighty. That's a fiver for your troubles," Gordon said.

"Aight then. Wait here, my friend. I will return."

The guy shuffled off and disappeared into the crowd. Gordon was worried that he might have gotten swindled, but he had no better prospects. He swayed and nodded to the music and after a couple tracks the guy returned.

"You got lucky. I hear these are 'rock and roll' rolls." The guy grabbed Gordon's left wrist with his clammy hand and dropped three pills into Gordon's palm. "Enjoy the trip."

"Catch you on the flipside," Gordon said, encouraged, rushing back to his friends. He handed one to Robert and one to Damian.

"It could take an hour to fully kick in. But then you're in for a ride," Damian said. "Okay, I'm going out there."

Damian danced with the crowd. An MC announced, "Good evening, Omaha! All the way from Brooklyn, New York in the houz y'all! On the ones and twos!"

The new DJ began with an ominous tone and ambient sounds as the fans hooped and hollered. Masterful screeching and scratching reverberated from the turntables.

And then, *boom*!

The bass and hyperactive beats took off, and the crowd responded with cheers and whistle blows. Track after track the beats drove on. Damian, Robert, and Gordon jumped up and down together. Gordon felt another rush come over him, a sensation that he was not ready for. The lights blurred, his heart raced, and he could not keep up with anything. He knew Damian was trying to talk to him but couldn't understand what he was saying. He didn't know where Robert went or what was going on. Damian and Debbie escorted them to the side, and they sat against the wall.

"Holy shit," he heard Robert say next to him.

"Are you guys feeling it?" Damian said.

"Oh yeah, definitely. Feeling something," Gordon said.

"Here, guys, take a load off. I'll be right here," Damian said to Robert and Gordon, and he kept dancing nearby.

Robert and Gordon sat against the wall and watched the show unfold. The biggest show was now taking the main stage inside them.

"Feel this," Robert said to Gordon, handing him his zippo lighter.

"What's going on? Cigarette?" Gordon said. He was overwhelmingly stimulated and perplexed.

"No, feel this lighter," Robert mumbled. Gordon felt the lighter with amazement. He touched his own arms. The hairs bristled with sensation. Gordon flicked the lighter on. He waved it in front of their faces. They were mesmerized instantly.

Debbie watched, smiling and twirling her pigtails.

"Here, sweetie. I can help. Just don't move. Stay still," she said. She pulled a pair of neon glowsticks out and waved them around Robert's head. She moved them with deft grace and liquidity to the pulse of the music.

"You're amazing, Debbie," Robert gushed. He held her hand and she rubbed his hair like a pet.

"Aw, thanks, Robert. Your turn," she said to Gordon, gently placing her hands on his cheeks to position his head. He was already stimulated by that contact. He watched as a stream of lights traced past his vision. The vision somehow caused a rush of euphoria to course through his body, overwhelming him. Then Debbie ran her hands across his forearms. There was nothing at all sexual about it, and yet it felt so good.

Debbie returned to Damian, leaving Gordon completely satisfied. Damian raised his fist in the air and banged his head to the music.

"Let's get up," Robert said.

Gordon could not quite follow the music, but he knew he enjoyed it. He loved it when the next track dropped, erupting the dance floor. Gordon threw his hands in the air and moved his feet, shuffling in place. He and Robert grabbed each other by the shoulders and jumped up and down. Damian joined them. They all had a group hug.

As the techno beats went on, the boys hoped the night would never end. Gordon felt a rush of high from the drugs that he had never experienced. He was consumed by a sense of oneness with the people at the party, as if each wanted to be a friend, and he was united with all of them. This rave experience was so bright and happy, accepting and loving and socially connected—while also dark, chemical, industrial, and underworldly. It was a spectrum of lights, unity, and aural bliss concocted in a lab by scientists and fallen angels.

Gordon was becoming more comfortable with his body. He found the raver who had sold him the rolls on the dance floor and expressed his highest gratitude. They bonded together and met new friends who were also rolling and getting wild on the dance floor. The gang got rowdy and joyously shoved each other around.

Damian walked up to Gordon and shouted in his ear, "I was just talking to Debbie, and she wants to leave soon. If you want to stay longer, I can find you and Robert a ride back to the motel."

"Man, I don't want to leave yet. This is great," Gordon said.

"Okay, I'll be back," Damian said.

Gordon watched an athletic man wearing shorts and, instead of a shirt, had wrapped himself with Christmas lights. The man danced liquid while the colorful lights blinked. He was an instant crowd pleaser.

Gordon, Robert, and the rest of the rowdy bunch raved on until early morning. The dance floor thinned out and they held on to the bitter end without feeling tired.

After they had secured the ride with a friend of Damian's, they found themselves relaxing in a motel room with several other ravers. Gordon never fell asleep. He sat on the floor, leaning against a chair while he came down. Damian walked over and handed him something secretly. Gordon turned away from the others to examine the small, orange bottle with the label torn off. The sun peeked over the horizon and cut through the window shades and shone on a small scrum of pills in the corner of the bottle.

"They're twenty-five a piece, and I might know where to get more," Damian said.

7/ GEOLOGY

Fall 1996

Studying is the combination of student and dying.
—Unknown

Gordon sat at his desk before Geology 101, a course recommended by Stuart at FarmTrepid as an easy A. Gordon was surprised to learn that the earth was in action, dynamic and ever-changing, and that the land only appeared static due to the relative brevity of human lives. He learned that tectonic plates were in motion, colliding with each other to create dramatic mountain ranges. Gordon felt like his own life was changing at a glacial pace and he was impatiently waiting. If only a new life could form, birthed out of the sea from fresh volcanic earth like the archipelagos of new islands.

Gordon snagged the *Daily Nebraskan* campus newspaper left behind on another desk and flipped through the pages of ads for bars & pubs and lecture note takers. Quotes of the Week about campus politics, the Board of Regents, and Nebraska football, comparing Tom Osborne to God, not in an "Oh Gee Whiz" type of way but in "The way I think of God is the way I think of Tom Osborne." Flip. A cartoon of Bob Dole and Bill Clinton debating and Ross Perot on the side with big dumbo ears. Conflicts in the Middle East, flip, Nebraska lost their first season football game since

1992. Flip. *Who cares about Husker football? That's Nebraskan blasphemy! Father, Son, and Holy Osborne.*

He looked carefully at a picture of young women in a fitness class at the Campus Recreation Center. Just a small and grainy picture. *Wait, is that Tonya?* He looked closer. *That is definitely Tonya!* And she was quoted saying, "The classes make exercising fun. We get help and motivation from the instructor. Plus, I know I can count on my friends to be there and support me."

Gordon discovered that Tonya was a freshman living on campus in Schramm Hall, a dorm adjacent to Harper Hall where Robert and Michael had lived.

"I have your exams graded. I'll hand those out and then we'll go over the lecture material from chapter seven on the hydrologic cycle." The lanky professor walked around the room, sliding the exams upside down onto desks. *Shit, a D-. Not good.* What could have gone wrong with his foolproof scheme of memorizing previous exams? Did they change the order or phrasing of the questions and answers?

The professor turned on his overhead projector and dimmed the lights. He sprayed a smudgy blank projector slide and wiped it clean, placing it over his first printed slide. He scribbled a wet green line as the coastline. Gordon's eyes got heavy. He heard something about "sediment" and "coastal erosion" before he faded out.

Gordon left the class knowing he was doing poorly and his life was taking a wrong turn. He tossed and turned at night, dreaming of incomplete assignments, failed tests. He invented gothic worlds of enormous iron and rust structures submerged in black water, a cold and vast bleakness. He was trapped in a labyrinth of subliminal caverns, paths, and characters, and other abstractions of failed coursework. Occasionally, he was a victorious hero in a beautiful forest fantasy. In the mist, he confessed true love to a lost soul, a love at last requited. He'd wake grasping the images, recently vivid but evaporating into sublimation, leaving no trace of memory.

Driving had always meant freedom and endless possibilities. Gordon headed eastward down O Street and turned south on 70th toward Holmes Lake.

He glanced at the digital dashboard of his hatchback, the futuristic styles of the '80s with sharp angles and showy technology that already seemed dated like a DeLorean. The flashing of orange digital lights, a speedometer of trapezoids that lit in fixed patterns, the tachometer bars that stacked up and disappeared on each upshift. The ten-inch kickers thumped, massaging his back and rattling the hatchback.

After he cruised Holmes Lake, he headed toward Tonya's old Havelock neighborhood. A Def Leppard song played, so he cast Tonya as a dreamy blond girl dancing in a rock music video next to his car. Then he imagined her a dancing pop star, like Debbie Gibson from the Electric Youth era. He envisaged Tonya wearing a jean jacket and white loop earrings, sun bleached brunette hair with bangs, a ponytail on top in a pastel scrunchy, and green eyes under contrasting tawny eyebrows. *Had she worn that hairstyle in the grade school yearbook photo in '85? Had she given me one of her color photos and written a note on the back?*

He decided to drive past Schramm Hall where Tonya was supposed to live. He was too rational to expect to run into her driving by, so would need a better plan to find her on campus. To an outsider, it might even be stalking. He had already lost interest by the time he arrived on campus, hindered by crowds of crossing pedestrians. As he drove back to the dorm, raindrops pelted his windshield, and his wipers smeared the streetlights.

{-----}

"So, Mr. Hamilton," the Dean said with his Great Plains drawl, not too drawn out, modest but proud, rural, and masculine. "It looks like we are here today because you are not passing Geology 101."

Gordon tried not to slouch in the chair opposite the Dean's large desk as he was subjected to this interrogation. "You're not messing with drinking too much? Or the drugs?" The Dean winced, clearly pained to even have to bring up drugs.

"No, not too much," Gordon said. "I go to parties with my friends, and we have drinks on the weekends."

"Well, boys will be boys."

"Right, yeah."

The Dean blinked several times. "The last question I'll ask is about your commitment to the university. I'll use one word. Apathy. Apathy, Gordon. Do you know what apathy means?"

"Yes, I do."

"Well, do you think it applies to you? I see that you're failing an easy course like Geology 101, and that you received a D in chemistry last semester. Typically, when this happens once, I'll see it happen again if we don't get it resolved. I want to make sure you're committed to your curriculum. Otherwise, you'll end up losing all your scholarships and grants. That your parents have worked hard for. Understood?"

"Yes," Gordon said, wishing he could crawl out a window.

"I am going to recommend that you're no longer enrolled in Geology 101, without a withdrawal, so you will get a refund on those credits and a clean transcript."

Gordon nodded and exhaled. *Good, one less class.*

8/ BUSINESS CONTACTS

Fall 1996

There are only two hard things in computer science:
cache invalidation and naming things.

—Philip Karlton, Principal Curmudgeon at Netscape

Todd Wallace used his father's connections to prospect for a business manager and accountant for their startup venture, and Barbara had come highly recommended. Gordon, Todd, and Robert sat in Barbara's cramped dining room, adjacent to the living room and the kitchen of the modest ranch home. The kitchen was busy with farmhouse wallpaper, paintings of roosters, rooster rags, earthy cabinets, beige linoleum countertops, an oven and microwave encased in a brick wall, and plants hung with macramé. A hutch displayed decorative plates and a collection of salt and pepper shakers. In the living room, two cats curled up and licked each other on a chair covered with a knitted blanket. There was a shelf of vinyl records, though the only albums Gordon could read were contemporary Christian singers Twila Paris and Amy Grant from before she went pop.

"I'm sorry, boys, I haven't even put my face on today," Barbara said, joining them from the kitchen. She wore a loose Hawaiian house dress and Golden Girls-style glasses, her hair dyed and permed. Barbara smiled cheerfully at the boys; her round cheeks pressed against her large frames. She placed a binder on the dining room table.

"Would you boys like something to drink? I brewed some iced tea and I have Pepsi and Mountain Dew in the garage?" Barbara asked before sitting.

"I'll take a Pepsi," Robert said. "Please."

"I'll have an iced tea, not sweetened, please," Todd said sheepishly.

Gordon merely smiled and shook his head politely.

Barbara lumbered off to get the drinks.

"So this is your bigshot contact?" Gordon whispered.

Todd scowled. "Shut up!" he hissed. "Do *you* know how to do the book-keeping? How about the corporation filings?"

"Todd, aren't you the CFO? Shouldn't that be your job?" Robert said sarcastically.

"Shhhh," Gordon said.

"I'm sorry, honey. I'm out of Pepsi," Barbara shouted from the garage. "I have Shasta and Rocky Top cola. Henry must have used his coupons. Would you boys like either of them?"

"I'll take a Rocky Top," Todd said.

"I'll have one too since you've gone to the trouble," Gordon said.

Barbara served the drinks and sat with them at the dining room table. She smiled at each of them. "So, how can I help you boys today?"

"Well, Barbara," Todd began, "we're starting an IT company— specifically a software company. We will build custom software products as well as serve customers with various computer programming needs."

"Oh, honey, I don't know the first thing about computer stuff. My youngest son plays on the only computer around here. When he's on that computer in the evenings, somehow it ties up our phone lines. Then Henry gets upset."

"He must be using your modem through the phone line," Robert said.

"I know we have the AOL. Is that a good one?" Barbara asked.

"Uh, yeah, it's probably a good service for you," Robert said, shooting a look at Gordon. One could line up discarded AOL CDs across the entire state of Nebraska.

"Anyway, I can't help you with computers," Barbara said. "But if you boys want help with collectibles, I'd be delighted to tell you all about mine."

"You have quite the collection," Gordon said, his gaze landing on the numerous salt and pepper shakers.

Barbara laughed. "Oh, those are just a few of my salt and pepper shakers on display. My true passion are Beanie Babies. I have quite the collection."

She launched into an animated history about how she got started, first with just a few beady-eyed bears of various styles and colors. Then she splurged on bears of rarer and wilder color patterns. And then dogs, birds, rabbits, monkeys, orangutans, and even an unusual duckbilled platypus.

"And now—I'm hooked. I bet some of them are valued at over five thousand dollars. Don't tell Henry," she said conspiratorially, "but I've been rerouting our retirement savings into Beanie futures."

"Personally, I'm partial for the salt and pepper shakers," Todd said. "Anyway, as far as computers and technology are concerned, all three of us have computer programming experience and training. What we really need is help setting up a corporation, like an LLC or something. And, once we get started, someone who can do the accounting and payroll and all those things."

"Well honey, I know that many companies form a corporation or an LLC. I suppose an LLC would make the most sense for a business of your size and makeup. If you want more specific advice or help with filing, you should talk to an attorney."

Todd frowned. "But you can help with the accounting and payroll and everything?"

"Oh, certainly," Barbara said, nodding enthusiastically. "I'm a certified public accountant. I've been an accountant for well over twenty-five years. I've helped many small businesses like yours. Besides, we could really use the work. I've had to support the family since Henry hurt his back."

If she's a CPA, why didn't she say that in the first place? Instead of talking about her Beanie Babies and shaker collections. But anyway.

"We'll be the officers of the corporation," Gordon said, "I'll be the CEO, Robert will be the CTO, and Todd will be the CFO."

"Oh, well, my goodness! I'm surrounded by very important people," Barbara squealed.

The young men nodded. Gordon wished they had dressed in suits or something, rather than t-shirts and cargo shorts.

"As CFO, I'll be your main point of contact. I'll be working out these details as we file the corporation or LLC," Todd said.

"Well, goodness, how many employees will you have?" Barbara asked.

"It will be the three of us, plus five or so additional employees, primarily engineers. They'll be part-time, at least at first. We're starting out with quality over quantity."

"Oh, okay, that shouldn't be too much to handle as far as payroll. What's the name of your company? Have you set up a bank account?" Barbara asked.

"We'll get you all the pertinent details," Todd said.

"No rush boys, I'm in no hurry." She went to the kitchen. "Does anyone want some cookies? Oh, I have Fig Newtons too, well, the generic brand?"

After declining the offer of a snack, they departed Barbara's. The ride back home was quiet; Gordon was not concerned about the LLC or DBA. The crux of the problem was not that they hadn't chosen a name, it was that they had no product, no prospective customers, and no money. He had to get things on track. He was the CEO.

"That went well. Now we have a business manager and accountant," Todd said.

"Let's assume Barbara's a good accountant. But we're missing so much here. We need to start thinking of product ideas, sources of funding, and a company name. Does everyone have time for a brainstorming session?"

Todd nodded. "I'm in."

"Me too" Robert said. "Oh, I told Oliver that we'd hang out. Can we pick him up?"

"We all love our Frodo," Todd said.

"We need to do an offsite session, like a retreat, or something," Gordon said after they picked up Oliver.

"We could go to the driving range and hit some balls," Todd suggested.

"Perfect. And I've got something to, shall we say, improve our creativity," Gordon said, referring to a few sticky buds.

They went to Rusty's Funway Park, a family fun center offering goofy golf, go-karts, batting cages, and a driving range.

"Should we burn one down?" Todd asked. "Shit, we don't have a pipe or papers."

Robert dug through the garbage in the back seat and found an empty can of Rocky Top cola. He fashioned a pipe out of it by flattening one side and poking a few holes in it with a safety pin. He set the buds over the holes, lit it, inhaled from the can mouth, and passed it around to the others. Gordon could taste the caramel sweetness from the soda. As the smoke rolled out of the windows, a minivan pulled up next to them and a noisy brood of children emptied through the sliding door.

"Should we move?" Oliver asked.

"Frodo don't be paranoid, bro," Todd said.

Once they were done, they purchased a couple of one hundred-pound buckets of balls and made their way to the range, carrying the heavy buckets in pairs, one on each side, like pails of water. The lights shone down on the brown grass as the evening grew darker.

"Try to hit that truck out there," Todd said, laughing as an employee in a truck raced around the driving range.

"I can't hit the ball." Oliver swung wildly again, hitting the top of the ball so it bounced sideways. Robert took an easy, graceful swing carrying the ball straight over the 250-yard marker.

"How the hell did you do that?" Gordon asked.

Gordon took a wild swing, grunting and carrying through and spinning wildly, ending in a squatting position. The ball hooked dramatically right, bouncing off the netting screen in front of a tree line.

"I've got a wicked curveball," he said.

"Am I the only one who's played golf before? Don't try so hard," Robert said.

"My dad is always trying to take me golfing at the country club," Todd said. "Weren't we supposed to be talking about business ideas?"

"Yeah. A company name for starters," Gordon said.

"GordonSoft," Oliver suggested.

Gordon shook his head. "It doesn't have to end in *soft*."

"Should we know what our product is and name that first?" Robert asked after he took another graceful swing.

"We don't have a product yet," Todd pointed out.

"Does anybody want a corn dog?" Oliver asked. They all nodded. "You men keep working; I'll go get four dogs."

"The name needs to be something about innovation, or vision, or synergy," Gordon said. They tried brainstorming. Whatever one came up with, the other two didn't like. When Oliver returned with the corn dogs, Gordon felt both ravenous and relieved. Maybe some food would help them be more productive.

"What about using names from famous people in the history of science or computing?" Oliver said. "Isn't that how Pascal and Boolean were named?"

Robert nodded. "Good idea. How about Babbage? Hopper? Uh, Newton?"

"Babbage and Hopper are a little clunky," Todd said, "but Newton is good but maybe a little too mainstream."

"I can't think of that many famous names. But keep going Robert," Gordon said.

"Ada Lovelace?"

"Ha, sounds like a porn star," Todd said.

"Tesla, Galileo."

"Carl Sagan?" Oliver suggested tentatively.

"That's it!" Gordon shouted. "Sagan Software!" He looked at Robert and Todd, who were nodding. Oliver looked thrilled.

"A breakthrough!" Robert said. "We've got a name."

{-----}

Gordon found Jennifer alone in Robert's room, studying. Gordon had grown weary of girlfriends and freeloaders hanging around their house and wondered why Jennifer was there if Robert was not.

"Have you seen Robert?" he asked from the doorway.

Jennifer paused, thumbing through her textbook. "He'll be back soon. I'm just finishing up some homework and then I'm going home."

"It's not super important. I just wanted to talk to him about our new business venture."

"I can tell him you stopped by. I think it's great you're getting him to take a chance. Robert is the smartest person I know but he doesn't like trying new things. I can't even get him to try new food."

"So, you two are, uh, doing better now?" Gordon asked.

"Oh, yeah. I think so. Robert isn't always the best at communicating his feelings. We have our spats here and there, but we're doing good."

"He's been much easier to deal with lately, for me at least, so hopefully you two can work it out."

"Well, I care about him. And he cares about you too," Jennifer said.

"He worries about you, to be honest. He thinks you overextend yourself. He says you're always taking risks. Robert wants a job that challenges him. He's more about settling down and having a family than chasing money."

"Really," Gordon said. "Robert seems pretty career-driven to me."

"Maybe, but I've seen another side of him. We've talked about settling down in the country. We want to live on an alpaca farm. Did you ever pet an alpaca? They are sooooo cute, with their long eye lashes. Robert is helping me plan too. He wants cage-free chickens. He's so hokey, I love it."

"Robert is smart as hell. I'm lucky to have him on my side. And you too apparently," Gordon said.

"Speaking of— Becky says hi. I'm sure I could set you up."

"You had to slip that in."

"I'm just trying to help, Gordon."

"Maybe I don't need help."

"Don't get in a tizzy about it. Don't you want a girlfriend? I've just never seen you with anyone. I've heard you mention Tonya but I've never even met her. And I'm around here all the time."

"Yeah. Tonya and I grew up together. She was my childhood crush. She was the only girl I could talk to in junior high. Only one that would talk to me. I feel like there is a lifelong connection. She's perfect for me."

Why am I telling Jennifer all this?

"Nobody is perfect Gordon. Trust me. Why would you even want perfect?"

"Perfect for *me*."

"But how would you even know? How do you really know something is there unless you're together? Like as in living day-to-day stuff. Not a romantic crush."

"I know she's out there. I've seen her. I'm not giving up without trying."

"Well, you deserve someone. It's what everyone loves about you, Gordon, you're such a dreamer."

He was a dreamer. Enough people had said that about him. But he was determined to show that he would turn those dreams into reality.

9/ BUSINESS CONTACTS II
Fall 1996

Everybody's got to do what they've got to do.

—Tom Osborne

As Thanksgiving break approached, Gordon was carrying heavier concerns than naming their startup company. He resigned from FarmTrepid to focus on engineering work, then lost his grip on coursework to pour himself into the company startup. While Gordon's friends discussed spring semester enrollment, Gordon quietly, shamefully, grappled with failing out of college. He was past the point of no return. That meant no more scholarships, grants, or loans. He was not going to seek help from his parents under these conditions.

Gordon drove to his bank ATM and withdrew $40 from his checking account. He looked woefully at the balance on the statement receipt. Although he had saved money during the summer, this meager budget was not going to last.

What can I sell? Not my car, no way. I love my car. I need my car. I should start by changing my spending habits. Sneak into the dining hall. Mooch off rich friends.

He had been saving spare change in a coffee can on his dresser. On weekends he walked to the burger joint and ate off the $1 menu. For extra calories he took shots of ketchup from the white paper cups. Save the quarters, use up the dimes and nickels with a few pennies for tax. He collected cheap cans of food like bean soup, ravioli, anything hearty. His dorm had to be vacated by the end of the semester. Maybe he could squat in the house basement and pay them under the table until he got on his feet. If he didn't cause waves, they would appreciate help on rent.

When Gordon urged his executive team to explore more paying opportunities, Todd leveraged his father for more contacts. Gordon drove toward Todd's parents' house, passing opulent suburban estates with countless gables and wraparound driveways. He was struck with envy, admiring a glossy black Porsche 911 parked in a three-car garage. *You'll make it over to this side of the track. Some day.*

Todd's cargo shorts and a wifebeater belied the grandness of the entryway and foyer. Gordon admired the spacious room past a winding staircase, a grand piano, and large framed paintings on the walls.

"Let's go talk to my dad. He's probably downstairs," Todd said. Todd's father was relaxing on a sectional in the finished basement, watching a movie from an overhead projector. Denny Wallace was an older, gray-haired, more distinguished looking version of Todd. *He takes care of his appearance, unlike my middle-aged relatives. Hair styled neatly, clean shaven, in shape, wearing a collared golf shirt. No suspenders, beard, or flannel. No belly sticking out of a faded Huskers t-shirt.*

Denny Wallace rose to introduce himself and then led them to his sprawling rumpus room. He walked behind the bar and prepared two glasses of iced Cokes with lemons. *Wow, an authentic Irish pub with leather bar stools and a full-sized billiard table. They even have ice and a sink.* Denny poured himself a couple fingers of single malt scotch.

"Gary Stanley is an old friend of mine from college," he said from behind the bar. "He's an eccentric character. He's abrasive, arrogant, but also extremely intelligent. He said he's been working on a computer programming project. He has time on his hands and disposable income. His wife wears the pants, but don't tell him I said it."

"So, does he work?" Gordon asked. "And he knows about us? About Sagan Software?"

"Yeah, he works, if you wanna call it that," Denny said. "And yes, he's expecting a visit from you today. You know, I really admire what you guys are doing and want to support you however I can."

"Thanks Dad, we're outta here," Todd said. He looked at Gordon. "Let's bounce."

They pulled into Gary's house, a white stucco Spanish colonial style home with recessed arched windows, curved wrought iron, and Spanish tiles. Inside, the front rooms were ready for a magazine shoot, a southwest motif of Spanish paintings, Meso-American art, a fireplace with ornate tiles, oak flooring, and native woven rugs. Gary silently guided Todd and Gordon to his wing of the house, a guest bedroom repurposed as his office. The cluttered room was filled with boxes piled on boxes, file cabinets stacked with books and papers, and a desk in the far corner and a pro mini basketball hoop against the far wall.

Gary wore his favorite basketball jersey and a peppered mustache; the hair on his head was short, frizzy, and parted down the middle. If he was ever athletic, it was decades in the past. He pulled up two folding chairs for Gordon and Todd and then sat on his swivel chair at his desk and turned on his computer.

"So, Sagan Software, huh." Gary stared at his computer. "This dang computer takes so long to reboot. Can either of you explain to me what takes so long? Press what for BIOS? Why can't they make a computer that will just start right up?"

"Well—"

"Do you know that the national debt is over five trillion dollars? The cumulative deficit is way beyond control. You'll see serious problems with national debt in your lifetime. Do the math, what do you think that is per capita? It's spiraling into oblivion and will take society with it."

"Yeah, it's—"

"It's bad enough that the government is mortgaging your future. I sure hope I'm dead by then. It's these big government programs, social security, welfare, and all. These political hacks in Washington are wanting to tax everything and do nothing. All these handouts. And then you've got these intellectual elites trying to brainwash our students. You guys go to UNL?"

"Yeah, well, just—"

"Then you know what I mean. The faculty, the *intelligentsia*, are all leftwing liberals. Democrats, all of them. Oh, piece of . . . finally, it's starting up," Gary exclaimed. "So, anyway, in a nutshell, I'm taking all these securities data feeds, SEC filings, financials, trades, other market data, and storing them in a database. I've figured out how to populate the data from public filings and other sources. That's easy. On top of that, I'm developing new and proprietary formulas to forecast and calculate valuation. On the app side, I've just started building some screens to manage the settings and run common tasks."

"This is all done in Visual Basic?" Todd asked. "Access database for the back end?"

"Yes. Look here." Gary showed Gordon and Todd the screens, source code, tables, and data files, occasionally complaining under his breath at the computer. "Once I have all of this in the database, I can analyze the data and run it through algorithms."

"You're going to make money from this application by trading stocks with the data?" Gordon asked.

"Oh, heck no. I want a sure thing. I'm going to offer a paid license for the software and subscription fees for analysis and reporting. And then I'm going to pay out fees for license referrals. That way my subscribers have a sure thing too by bringing in more subscribers while growing my customer base."

Gary leaned back and swiveled, throwing his little rubber basketball through the hoop.

"Here's a free tip for my Future Business Leaders of America. It is too dang hard to invent. And even if you have a new concept for a product, someone else will do it better than you and take all the business anyways. If you want to make money, you need to get closer to the money. Put yourself right in the middle of transactions and always take a cut."

"Did you do all this yourself? It looks good, really," Todd said.

"Don't act surprised, but sure, thanks. I'm self-taught. But now I need help. I've laid the groundwork for the application. It's all there. And now I need to focus my time on developing the business side."

"Well, I'm sure we can have someone help you with the programming."

"Oh, shoot. The wife's home. She's here already?" Gary hunkered down like a guilty cat. He shuffled toward his outside door and ducked. "Is she home? I'll be outside. Can you see if she's home? Someone, go look for me."

Keys hit a table. The door swung open. The wife was standing in the doorway in a pants suit. "Hey, Gary. Did you not get the trash taken out in time?"

Gary threw the basketball to her. Or, at her.

"Oh, hello, how are you all?" the wife asked Gordon and Todd with a forced smile. She left before they could answer.

"More free advice. Don't ever get married," Gary said.

{-----}

"It's all visual basic 4.0, really long procedures, like thousands of lines long, and heavy on relational databases, some scripting," Todd explained. "It's not done properly, but it's quite impressive that it actually all works. It's like he figured it all out on his own. Well, I guess he did."

"Who knows Visual Basic? Robert, you could pick that up," Gordon said.

"I did some old school BASIC when I was a kid. That's it. Anyhow, I'm still working at FarmTrepid on top of seventeen credit hours. I don't have time for this one," Robert said.

"Doesn't Stuart know VB? Hasn't he bragged about it?" Gordon asked.

"He doesn't fit our company culture. Not that tool, no," Todd said.

"Settle down, Todd. We're professionals," Robert said.

"You knew we were going to hire help," Gordon added.

"Fine, but who's talking to him?"

"I'll talk to him. I know him well enough. I think he's still working at FarmTrepid." Gordon was desperate to make anything work.

"This Gary guy has money. Let's just give Gary an hourly programmer rate. Then Sagan Software can bill out Stuart hourly," Todd said. "Can we offer Stuart two dollars an hour more than FarmTrepid? How could he say no?"

I can negotiate from both sides, get a great margin, and take a good cut for myself. I need the money bad. He'd talk with him today.

"Good job, CFO. Now Robert, as CTO, all you need to do is make sure the technical design is feasible."

"That's the bomb, Gordon," Todd said. "And now that we've got that all figured out, what's up with this house party tonight? Who's gonna be there?"

"Damian and Debbie, and—"

"Debbie? Is she the one that Damian brought over to my parents' house? She's trailer trash, dog."

"That's rude, Todd. Have some kind of respect," Robert said.

"Well, it's true. She was like admiring everything, all uncomfortable and stuff, like she'd never been in a real house."

"She's Damian's girl. And she's never harmed a fly," Gordon said.

"I think she's charming and sweet," Robert added.

Todd shuddered. "Just don't bring her and her dirtbag friends around my place."

"Not a problem," Gordon said. "So, who's going to drive?"

10/ LINES OF BUSINESS

Winter 1996

Your eyes will see strange sights,
your mind will imagine confusing things.

—Proverbs 23:33

The house was sparsely populated when they arrived, unfinished and unfurnished, not in that new smell way, more like an incomplete remodel job from decades past. A large, intimidating man leaned over the pool table. He measured and shot. He had tan skin and thick black hair and a braided goatee, and he wore a white sleeveless shirt and black jeans with a silver chain connecting to his wallet. Gordon, Robert, and Todd talked amongst themselves in the mostly vacant front room.

These men looked more like Hell's Angels than Nebraska college students.

"Should we leave?" Todd asked quietly. "This looks sketchy."

"Relax Todd, I think there's a keg. I can go get us some beers," Robert said, and took off out a side door before Todd could respond. He returned a few minutes later balancing several red plastic cups of beer. They had not seen Damian or Debbie yet.

They stood in a huddle with their cups. "Are you going to follow up with Gary about Stuart?" Todd asked.

"I'm glad he took what you offered," Robert said.

"It went well enough," Gordon said. "He took the offer. I just told him that we'd pay fifty cents more an hour than FarmTrepid and that he could flex his schedule."

Their attention was pulled to the pool table; Damian had just walked in and was talking to the towering man playing pool. Damian looked over at them, gave them the peace sign, and then a thumbs up to the large man. Gordon thought this meant they were in.

He finished his beer and left the group conversation in search of a bathroom. He walked down the dim hallway and opened a door—to his surprise, the bathroom was already occupied by Damian and Debbie.

"Sorry, I was looking for the restroom," Gordon said.

"Come on in. Shut the door. Shut the door," Damian said intensely.

Gordon averted his eyes. Then he spotted a mirror on the sink counter with a small rock of cocaine.

"Bolivian marching powder. Do you want to party with us?" Damian asked.

Debbie smiled and crinkled her nose.

To Gordon, the white powder seemed more criminal than marijuana and pills combined. On the other hand, he had been terrified at first of marijuana only to realize that it was mostly harmless. Still, he couldn't help but feel extremely nervous and scared. Damian pulled out a razor and broke up the chunks and carved out three lines.

"You can go first. We've had a head start," Damian said, handing him a rolled-up bill. Gordon took it and leaned forward without a plan. "No, you want to plug your other nostril like this. No. Just, just use two hands then. And don't blow it everywhere—"

And before Damian could explain it, Gordon had already snorted two of the lines.

"Wait, those others are for us," Damian said, then cleaned up the remaining line with his nose. "No harm. Beginner's luck. I'll make us new ones, baby."

As Damian and Debbie sniffed up a couple lines of white powder, Gordon took in his surroundings. *The bathroom looks neat, like it has never been used. Look, there's an empty space where a shower can go. I'm very fortunate to be here.*

"I thought marijuana was getting high. This is *real* getting high," Gordon said, feeling the surge. "Is it safe? Safe, like marijuana?"

"Is cocaine safe, Gordo? I'm not sure I can say *that*," Damian prattled. "Gordo, can I call you Gordo? What I can tell you for certain is that we have been lied to by the media. We have been told lies by the authoritarian capitalist regime. With propaganda. We've been lied to by our parents and the government. With the war on drugs, a war against our own people, our prison systems are filled with drug dealers instead of violent criminals. We are the children of '80s, of the Reagan era, Gordo. The trickle down, Reaganomics, '80s Wall Street."

"Wall Street?" Gordon asked.

Did Gordon Gekko do cocaine? Were the '80's Wall Street guys doing cocaine too?

"The rich white guys are doing cocaine without consequences," Damian said, as if he read Gordon's mind. "The crack epidemic is just a few miles away in the ghetto. In the slums, your dad's not a junk bond salesman, Gordo, no, he's a junkie, and he left your crackhead mom with your brother and sister to fend for themselves. Meanwhile, Nancy Reagan is sitting in her ivory tower. In the White House. Gordo, Nancy's the worst. We are children of Nancy Reagan's *Just Say No* campaign. Just say no? That's the authoritarianism I'm talking about. Why not talk to your children about it like they have brains and can rationalize on their own? If you tell them just to say no and they go and get high and nothing that bad happens, then they'll know they've been lied to. We've been lied to, Gordo."

Gordon had been nodding, captivated by Damian's diatribe. He felt a rush to his heart. The conversation resonated in his chest.

"But what I'm asking," Gordon was struggling to grasp his original question and whether it had been answered. "What I'm asking . . ."

"Go on, it's okay." Damian licked his lips.

"So, if marijuana is . . . is it more safe than cocaine because it's natural?"

"Oh, I love this question, Gordo. Thank you for asking me. I learned from junior high health class about all hard drugs and where they came from. That's where the fascination grew, Gordo, where it was planted."

Debbie, clearly, was on a different frequency. Gordon watched as she kept trying to stand on her toes.

"What makes something natural?" Damian continued. "Marijuana is a plant that grows in nature and humans have been growing it and smoking it for who knows how long. Cocaine comes from coca leaves from the coca plant that grows naturally in South America and the South American Indians chewed on the leaves for a pick me up for centuries before the white man arrived like aliens on horseback. So, who's to say what is natural and not?"

"But cocaine has been transformed, it's been synthesized by humans, so we're not taking it in a natural form," Gordon said.

"So has a chocolate bar. Chocolate naturally comes from cacao beans that grow on trees. But, Gordo, would you not rather have a chocolate candy bar in the transformed state than chew on some lousy beans?"

"Yes, yes!" Gordon said.

"Besides, nature does terrible things too. Think of all the natural poisons, I mean, plants and snakes and frogs. Frogs, Gordo! Did you know the most toxic animal is some South American frog?! I'm gonna call you Gordo. Besides, aren't we part of nature too? Good and bad. And if humans are part of nature, then what we create is natural, by the transitive property, right?"

"Maybe you're right. That's crazy! Maybe. I don't know." Gordon had never considered it that way. But it made sense.

"He's got to be right, man," Debbie said. "Damian speaks the truth. Gordo, my mother wanted me to be a ballerina. But I quit practicing. I quit dancing like I quit everything. Not that my mom can talk." Debbie held her hands up and tried to stand on her toes again.

"So, if humans are part of nature, then everything we make is natural, and your question doesn't make sense," Damian said. "Now this is what blows my mind, Gordo. The only reason these drugs work is because they act as receptors in your brain, causing the release of dopamine or serotonin or whatever. So, think of it this way, Gordo. These plant chemicals and human brains share like a symbiotic bond. They are keys that fit perfectly into the keyholes in your brain. The brain keyhole had to be there in the first place for the chemical to fit in and turn the ignition. That is nature on its most microscopic and predestined level."

"So, your brain is designed to receive these drugs?"

"Yes! Cocaine is the key designed by nature's locksmith to fit your brain's keyhole. It's a symbiotic miracle between plant and animal, like fruit to be picked. Like peyote mushrooms that ignite our brains to create spiritual journeys. Shamans use peyote to talk to spirits, have visions that they painted on walls centuries, even millenniums, or is it millennia, before Chris Columbus."

"Mind-blowing, man," Debbie said, spinning around. A cocaine fueled pirouette.

"Literally, mind blowing," Gordon said.

"Speaking of blow," Damian said, carving out three more thick rows, like miniature crop rows to be nose harvested. They all partook. "So, you want to be a tech entrepreneur. Good for you, Gordo. You know, I'll probably end up doing lab work of some kind. Yeah! I told you that already. At Wednesday Night Session. Yeah. But the real reason I'm in chemistry, Gordo, let me tell you about my dream. My dream is to design a new drug. A new recreational drug, I mean."

"That's a great idea!" Gordon said.

Gordon recalled his need to use the bathroom and had completely lost track of time. Damian rubbed his gums with his powder finger. Gordon brushed his teeth with his index finger too.

"You're so smart, Damian," Debbie said as she pirouetted.

"Is there another bathroom?" Gordon asked. "I have to go."

"You can just go here. I won't watch." Debbie looked down at the toilet in front of her and snickered.

"Yeah, Gordo, just across the hall. The master bedroom has a spare bathroom that you can use," Damian said.

On the way back, Gordon searched for his friends but didn't find them. He returned to the bathroom and found the dark-haired man from the pool table there with Damian and Debbie.

"No, he's cool," Damian said. "Gordon, meet Br—I mean, meet Dino. Dino, this is Gordo. Gordo goes to college with me."

They bumped knuckles.

"*Gordo* means *fat* in Spanish," Dino said, caressing his braided goatee.

"Actually, I go by Gordon."

"Really?!"

Dino handed something to Damian, gave Gordon a nod, and left the bathroom. Damian unfolded something in his hand and pulled out a large roll of bills. Gordon's eyes popped out.

"Gordo, there's a lot of *dinero* in *yayo*," Damian said.

That's just what I need. I'm that desperate. Seems risky, possibly dangerous. No better time to take a risk.

"You need any help with that?" Gordon asked.

"Help with what?"

"With your risky business. In selling merchandise."

"Oh, Gordo! You want to get into the game?" Damian asked, frowning in deep contemplation. "You need to be careful with the white powder. You don't want to have anything to do with that business."

Gordon could not find it in his pounding heart to tell him that he was dropping out of college. And that he had no money.

"Are you sure?" he asked.

"I've got a better idea for you. One that would be perfect for an unassuming college student like yourself," Damian said.

Gordon licked his lips and nodded. He was up for it.

"Call me on this phone line. I'll arrange a meeting with Dino. For a more suitable time and place."

{-----}

Gordon cleared his throat while he waited for Gary to pick up the phone.

"Hello, is this Gary?" he said, feeling awkward asking.

"This is he," Gary answered.

"Hi, this is Gordon Hamilton, CEO of Sagan Software. I just wanted to call to, uh, touch base with you on how things are going with your project. How is Stuart doing?"

"He looks like a kid, a high school kid," Gary said. "I expected someone more experienced and mature than him. But he's getting the work done. Sometimes I ask him a simple question and he gives me a scholarly lecture."

"Well, he's nineteen. He's a character, but he's got a lot of programming experience."

"He's only nineteen?! As in, last year he was getting his ear pierced at the mall Claire's for his eighteenth birthday?"

Gordon let out a little laugh. "If you want to meet up to discuss anything, or if there are any issues with Stuart, just let me know. He has a typical computer programmer personality, not a bad thing."

"No, no, he gets the work done. He said his last name's Sandberg, is that German? Or do you know if Stuart, uh, is he Jewish?"

"I don't know. Does that make a difference?"

"No, I'm just asking. Not judging. There are plenty of ingenious Jews. Levi Strauss, Bob Dylan, and Einstein obviously. Did you know how many Hollywood stars changed their names: Tony Curtis, Kirk Douglas, even the Warner Brothers?"

"What about the Warner Brothers?" Gordon had no idea what this had to do with Stuart.

"The Warner Brothers were Jewish immigrants," Gary said. "Not just Warner Brothers, but Fox, and MGM, too. They changed their names to sound American, to sound Anglicized—"

"I love the Warner Brothers cartoons. Watched them all the time as a kid, so did my mom."

"Sure, you did. So, is that all for today?" Gary asked. He seemed impatient with small talk.

"We'll have Robert, our CTO, review the work next month when we all get together," Gordon said.

"He's Chief Technologist, huh. How old is he, twenty?"

"Yes."

Gary groaned.

"Last thing," Gordon said. "I just wanted to make sure you received the latest invoice."

"Yeah, I have. Sagan Software, you guys are awfully proud of your services. It's a little steep, but I suppose you boys are worth it. Am I supposed to send it in the mail, or can I just pay you cash, hand delivered? I strongly prefer cash, please."

"I'll check with Barbara, our accountant, but either way should be fine." Gordon was relieved by the news of income and strongly preferred cash himself. He would check with Barbara right away on the deposit. "We really appreciate your business," he added.

Gary hung up the phone. No goodbye.

{-----}

Gordon pulled into a gravel parking lot outside of town. It was a remote area with old softball diamonds, a bike trail, and a forlorn tetherball pole. Damian and Dino were already there, leaning against a 1965 Ford Galaxie like up-and-coming gangsters. They greeted Gordon, bumping knuckles.

Gordon looked up at Dino, whose face was expressionless behind his dark sunglasses.

"You look clean cut," Dino finally said. "That's good for business. So, you are into E?"

"You mean ecstasy?" Gordon asked.

"Yeah, MDMA, Vitamin E. You're part of the rave scene, right?" Dino tugged on his goatee braid.

"I've been to a couple raves with Damian."

"Wait, that's not what I heard." Dino shot a look at Damian. "This doesn't sound right; I thought you said he was legit. Like this guy was big into the rave scene and shit."

"Don't worry, Dino, I'll take care of that. Omaha style," Damian said. "I'm vouching for him. He's legit."

Dino looked at Gordon and then back to Damian.

"How tall are you?" Gordon asked.

"He's six foot eight," Damian answered quickly. "And he does not like being asked."

Dino peered down at him through his shades. Gordon smiled weakly. *A really stoic personality, this one.*

"So, start with twenty-five, and we'll see how he does," Dino said to Damian. He looked at Gordon. "Are you ready to start?"

"Yes, I brought cash." Gordon reached into his pocket, his hands trembling so much that the bills were shaking. *Play it cool.*

"Man don't pull that out here," Dino snapped. "Let's get into the Galaxie."

"Sorry," Gordon said. He hoped Dino hadn't noticed his wrecked nerves. Damian and Gordon climbed into the backseat while Dino sat up the front. He turned his large frame around toward them.

"Twenty-five at twenty is five hundred. You got five bills?" he asked.

Gordon did the quick math and hesitated.

"You can get thirty out of these easily. Maybe more, that's up to you," Damian said.

"Once you prove yourself, we can talk about better numbers. I take the risk; I get the reward. You know what I'm saying?" Dino said.

"Okay, yeah, let's do it." Gordon was still shaking but relieved to get it over with so he could hurry up and get out of the car. He handed Dino the cash. That had depleted his savings and checking accounts and had required him to even dip into Sagan cash.

Gordon waited, trying to play it cool, shifting in the seat.

I should get the merchandise now, right?

"Don't you have something for me?" Gordon asked.

Dino shook his head. "I didn't bring anything today. I wanted to make sure this was on the level. I'll come to you, man. You tell me where to find you and I'll find you."

Gordon's anxiety swelled. *What is going on? Am I getting swindled? Ripped off?*

"Gordo, relax, man." Damian patted his shoulder. "I've made this connection in good faith. Dino's good for his word. We go back, old school."

"I still officially live in the dorm for the rest of the semester, so I guess you could find me there," Gordon said.

"That won't work. I'll call you and arrange something else."

"Okay." Dino had all his money. All he could do now was wait and hope he came through.

{Part 2}

11/ THE SECRET OF MY SUCCESS
Winter 1996-97

Your best and wisest refuge from all your troubles is in your science.

—Ada Lovelace

Sagan Software steadily grew as they acquired more paying clients for web development, hosting, and other programming projects. Gary's software venture looked promising too, with subscriptions on the rise. In terms of cash flow for Sagan Software, Gary had a long backlog and a seemingly unlimited budget. It was time to bring some others on.

Gordon, Robert, Todd, and Vikram Singh walked through the Historic Haymarket District area southwest of campus, passing several more turn-of-the-century brick warehouses renovated into shops and office space. They passed an Italian restaurant and headed straight for a dive bar that did not card early in the day.

"Vik, you're a terrific webmaster and systems admin, *and* IT generalist," Robert said.

"And we'll pay way better than FarmTrepid," Gordon added. "You can make your own hours and we'll pay you even more money. You can stay in school too."

Vikram nodded thoughtfully. "How much would the pay increase be?"

"How much more do you need?" Todd asked.

As they talked, the bartender poured several clear liquors into a fish tank and colored it with sweet and sour mixers. Robert carried the sloshing fish tank to a table where they guzzled it through long bendy straws. The tavern featured the typical tipsy pastimes like pinball, darts, pool, and the lamentable open mic night. The most infamous tradition in the tavern's twenty-plus years of service was to never, under any circumstances, clean the restrooms.

"How much do you charge to build and host a website?" Vikram asked. "Like just a single business website with the basics."

"That's trade secrets, Vik. And you haven't even agreed to sign on," Robert said.

"Oh, screw it! I'm in." Vikram looked down as if already regretting his decision.

Gordon clapped him on the back. "Welcome to Sagan Software."

"Let's drink to that!"

They crossed their long straws in the air like the four musketeers. All for one and one for all.

"Who else is on board?" Vikram asked.

"So far?" Gordon said. "Stuart. Yeah, just Stuart Sandberg. He's already committed to a project. And we have a few temporary hourly employees, mostly interns, doing web programming."

"I think Stuart is all right. He's a good programmer."

Todd looked at Vikram, scoffing. "Stuart, mister future volcanologist. He's a tool."

"Why would you disparage your own employee?"

"Vikram, are we talking about the same Stuart?"

Before he could respond, a stranger walked up to their table, staring vacantly. The man turned his blank, inebriated eyes to the fish tank before his bloodshot stare landed on Vikram.

"Why you wearing . . . Why do you've got a goddamn rag on your head?"

"It is not a rag. It's a turban," Vikram said patiently.

"You know my uncle was killed during the desert war. He fought against the Arabs in, uh, the Muslims in Desert Storm," the stranger rambled.

"But I'm not a Muslim. I'm a Sikh. Different religion. My parents are Indian, not Arabic, from Punjab region of India—"

"Oh, they fought with all of them in Kuwait," the stranger continued.

"Hey bro, why don't you mind your own business and leave our friend alone," Robert said, his voice rising. "You heard me. Just get the fuck away from our table!"

"Or what?" the stranger asked.

Another man had approached the drunk stranger and was trying to pull him away. "I'm sorry. Is my friend bothering you?" The stranger's shouts faded into the dinge and the Sagan party resumed.

"Some friend he is," Robert said.

{-----}

Gordon's phone rang Monday morning. His head felt like it was infested with packrats. He could not remember exactly what happened before they were kicked out of the tavern after the altercation.

"Uh, hello," Gordon mumbled, instantly regretting that he even answered his phone.

"You sound like I just woke you up. It's almost eleven o'clock, for Pete's sake." It was O'Neill from FarmTrepid.

"I had the morning off. Slept in," Gordon said, turning over on the lumpy futon mattress.

"Well, I wanted to call you and ask if you'd please quit poaching my programmers. First Stuart and now Vikram?"

"He told you already?"

"Handed me his two weeks' notice this morning," O'Neill said.

"Hmm." In his hungover and befuddled state, Gordon really had nothing to say to O'Neill. He got up and stumbled into the bathroom.

"Listen, Gordon, I do wish you the best. What do you call your new business?"

"Sagan Software," Gordon said. He observed a colorful living organism flourishing in the toilet.

"Gordon, I'm just pulling your leg. I mean no ill will, but I do need to retain talent. Please, as a personal favor, if you could give me a friendly call before you hire someone else away. Communication is all I'm asking for. And, you never know, someday we may do business together," O'Neill said, chuckling.

"No problem."

"Gordon, you're young and talented. I've been doing this for a while, and I'm here if you ever need someone."

"Thanks, O'Neill," Gordon said. His call waiting beeped. "I may take you up on that. It's not like I know what I'm doing all the time. I have a call on the other line I need to take." He said goodbye to O'Neill and switched to the other line.

"Hey, it's Damian. Are you in on the rave in Omaha? This Saturday?"

"What? Uh, yeah sure, when am I going to get my—"

"I'll get you your—I'll return the sports gear that Dino borrowed from you, uh, to you on the way. I'll meet you at the house at around seven." Damian said.

"Cool, see ya then. Peace."

{-----}

After the rave, Gordon slept in, timeless, as if day were night and night was day, wide awake in his dreams yet drowsy in awakened periods. He felt disconnected from the world and wanted to be alone. He covered up, hoping to fall back into his everlasting dreams, where he felt a gap in his mind where the pain should have been. He imagined the gap would gradually fill back in, like a footprint in the sand. Unlike his first bad hangovers from drinking, he was not inflicted with bodily sickness or a sharp headache. He crawled out of bed and put on some sweatpants and a t-shirt and sprawled on the couch in the dark basement, finding solace in a series of *Quantum Leap* reruns.

Later, he drove to the local quick shop for a fountain drink to kickstart the day. Tonya had appeared off and on in his strange dreams. *I should still be looking for Tonya. What would I even say to her if I did find her?*

This was hardly any different than when he was fourteen years old and contemplating whether to walk up to her house. He planned to ask Tonya if she would go out with him. Gordon had recently been plagued with acne made worse by greasy finger squeezing, digging with tweezers, and lancing with needles. He promised himself that once his face cleared that summer, he would walk up to her house, knock on the front door, and confidently ask her to go out with him.

Gordon slid in a new alternative rock CD. Four chord rock. He turned it up. He thought about how to find Tonya. He looked through his contact list for underclass high school friends who might have her number. That group of sophomores and juniors who used to hang out with Tonya. Maybe one of them knew how to contact her.

I have Worthless Brad's number. I bet he knows how to reach her. Maybe Worthless Brad has a purpose.

Inside the convenience store he heard rock and roll music. He smelled burnt coffee and cheap vanilla cappuccino garbage. And cinnamon rolls. Again, rolls. He reminisced of his Saturday high. *The slushie machines are rolling over, turning like records, rolling. I've got twenty-five rolls. I could get thirty dollars each in the right crowd. I'll need a plan.*

{-----}

"What is the deal with that kid? I told Stuart repeatedly that I'm only storing raw data in the database. He added new tables and is storing data from aggregate functions and calculations. I told him that all statistics will be calculated on the fly. He has no idea about the analysis." Gary leaned back in his swivel chair and bounced his rubber basketball against the wall.

"I see. Did he happen to say why he wanted to do that?" Gordon asked.

"Well, Stuart thinks it will improve performance. He said he was building a cache in the database." Gary paused. "You ever heard of that?"

"It's not the worst idea. But I'll remind him that you make all final decisions. He can share ideas, right? He just needs to run them by you and let you make the call."

"That's right, Gordon. And, hey, what is the deal with him anyway? Is he, is he a queer or something? He kind of acts like a dandy. And he dresses like Gene Kelly with a frock coat and all. Like he's going on stage in costume or something. He's a strange kid."

"I think he's trying to dress to appear more adult," Todd said. "He's just a weirdo."

Gary gave him a stern look. "I'm friends with your family, Todd. You were all raised Christian. Your father Denny is a good Christian. I see him at church every Sunday."

"Yes, I know all that."

"Anyway, I'll let you sort that out with him."

"The gay thing?" Todd asked.

"No. Criminently, no! The database thing." Gary shuddered. "Just please get him to take better direction from me."

"Yeah, we'll take care of that," Gordon said.

"Thanks. Anyway. You guys want any sushi? My wife ordered way too much. There are two extra rolls in the kitchen," Gary said.

Rolls. Again with the rolls. I have pills to move. Another rave, another dollar.

"Is it raw?" Todd asked.

"Of course. This is great food, Todd. From the best Japanese restaurant in town," Gary said.

"That's gross." Todd looked horrified. "I can't eat uncooked fish. Is that even safe?"

Gordon recalled asking Damian if cocaine was safe. *Is it safer than eating raw fish in Nebraska?*

"People eat this stuff all the time," Gary said. "Go ahead. It'll grow hair on your chest. And hey, Todd, you know if poker night is at your house this month?"

"I think so. I'm not sure. You know I don't live at home with my parents anymore."

"Tell your mom to make her delicious queso dip again," Gary said. He leaned toward Gordon and whispered, "You know, in college, Todd's mom was quite a catch."

If I caught Todd's mother, I would throw her back in.

"Speaking of database tables . . ." Gary said, "Did you two know that there are banks in Omaha, major financial institutions, storing year date fields as two-digit numbers rather than four-digit numbers? There are going to be some major problems when the year 2000 comes along."

"I see. How do you know so much about that?" Gordon asked.

"Because my wife is a banking executive. A senior vice president, although banks give everyone and their mother a VP title. How do you think we afford this nice house? On sales of subscription revenues from this software venture?" Gary laughed sarcastically.

"The year 2000 problem. That's interesting. You know, that is something Sagan can help with," Todd said.

"But it's going to be the national debt that destroys this country," Gary went on, as though he didn't hear Todd. "Or a massive volcano could destroy Seattle or Wyoming, or a tsunami could wipe out the California coast. Imagine terrorists getting their hands on nuclear weapons or bombing a major city center. You boys are still young. I'd still be prepared if I were you. I'm stockpiling. I've already started planning construction on my bunker. I'm getting ready."

Talk about a cache, Gary is caching for the end of days.

"Oh yeah? A bunker? Where's that going to be?" Todd asked.

"Like I'd tell you guys." Gary shook his head. "But for the next few years, I'm optimistic. I'm bullish on the stock market. Thanks to my new analysis and formulas, I have the data to support that. The DOW will hit 10,000 someday soon, maybe 20,000 or even 30,000 in your lifetime. Buy some Intel or AMD stocks or any blue-chip stocks. Buffett is bullish on the S&P too. You can't go wrong."

{-----}

Rave parties followed in Omaha and then Kansas City. Gordon's rolls went like hotcakes. In Omaha, the first twenty-five sold quickly, so he called Dino to get a hundred more for Kansas City, and those flew off the shelves before the night was over. Another hundred more here and there and then thousands. Gordon was handing out digits like a stock ticker.

He strutted the Lincoln streets with swagger. A new black leather coat and sunglasses. Counting good fortunes. Scrolling his contact list. He would whip out the cell phone and extend the plastic antennae. Another raver contact, another hundred rolls here or there. Talking in code. Meeting strange people in bars and house parties. Getting hooked up as the new hook up.

This time it was Dino calling.

"What's up man?" Gordon said.

"How many points do you think you'll score this weekend?" Dino asked, in code.

"I'm not sure." Despite his financial success so far, Gordon knew that this life in the fast lane could very easily catch up with him. He didn't want to be so naïve to think that this might just keep going on forever.

"C'mon, player," Dino coaxed.

"I may not even play this weekend. I'm kind of sore from the last game. I might just sit out this time."

"You're not sure? What do you mean? How about just a few hundred points?"

Gordon felt that he was at a crossroads. To choose the right path, and take a step back, or walk away. He would have to confront Dino's resistance and pressure. Or even worse. On the other hand, Gordon could go with the flow. More risk, more reward. Life in the fast lane.

"Okay," he relented. "I'll bet I can score seven hundred points this weekend."

"I'm a fan. I'll come by and pick you up for the game out back," Dino said.

{-----}

The crew took to the backyard again for their Wednesday Night Session, grooving to the music, burning branches and trash from the neighborhood. Gordon signaled for Robert to follow him inside. They went upstairs to Robert's room and Gordon shut the door.

"I know you're going to find this out somehow and I'd rather you hear it from me," Gordon started. This was not a conversation he was eager to have but it had to come out some time. "I'm selling E. Not a major player, but big enough. It will make a difference for us financially. It's going to help us get Sagan Software where it needs to be. Only in the short run. I know how to step away from it when it's time," he added.

Silence.

"Robert, say something."

Robert took a deep breath and waited several more seconds. "This is risky," he finally said. "Maybe even dangerous. I don't like it at all. But I can't blame you, Gordon. I'm not a hypocrite. You've hooked me up so it's not like I didn't have a clue."

"Todd can't know. Don't ever tell Todd or anyone else from Sagan anything. I'm going to need to take over finance. I'll work with Barbara on the accounting. Trust me, Rob. I'll figure it out."

"So you're like . . . like drug dealing and money laundering?" Robert looked up at the ceiling and then closed his eyes. "This is not why we started Sagan Software. Carl Sagan deserves better."

"Don't be dramatic," Gordon said.

"You know, Carl Sagan passed away in December."

"He died? That's too bad. I didn't know."

"And this is how we honor him. We know better."

"No, Rob. And don't worry about it. I'll take care of it. Just have my back with Todd on needing me to take over the finances. I'm the CEO, right? We'll praise Todd. I'll take over finance and give Todd the title of Head of Sales and Marketing. You know Todd. Just make it about his ego, and that'll keep him occupied," Gordon said.

"I'll support you, buddy. But you have to stay on the level with me, no matter how bad. And don't get us in any real trouble."

Gordon held his hand out. "I promise."

They shook hands. Gordon patted Robert on the shoulder.

"Let's get back before we draw any suspicion," Robert said.

12/ SUMMER BREEZE

Summer 1997

Do not let play interfere with work. Work hard, and when you play, play hard.
—Theodore Roosevelt

"So, you would like to hire us to develop a website for your company. And this website will be used to buy and sell boats?" Gordon and his team sat in the Omaha conference room, dressed in business casual.

"Yes." Hank Sherman, the sharply dressed Omaha businessman, nodded. "Expressly, I will offer a website to my clients allowing them to list their boats for sale online. They register on our site and then we provide them with a marketplace to list their boats . . . At a commission, of course."

"Why boats?" Vikram asked.

Hank raised his eyebrows. "Really? Who doesn't like boating?"

"I love boating," Robert said.

"Let me get a show of hands. Who would rather be on a boat right now than sitting in this conference room?" Hank asked. He raised his hand. Robert, Gordon, Vikram, and Todd followed suit. Hank's lawyer looked up from his legal pad and raised his hand too.

"Let me recast the question," Vikram said. "Why boat sales in Omaha? Why not real estate or farm equipment or other assets more commonly traded in the Omaha, Nebraska area?"

Gordon was surprised and envious that Vikram was asking all the good questions. He was the introverted sysadmin, not one of the business leaders.

"Well, here's the thing, Vikram. The website will not be exclusively for customers in Omaha. The website will be online and accessible to everyone in the USA."

"Duh," Todd said under his breath.

"So, Hank," Gordon said, wanting to come up with a good question of his own. "What market segments are you targeting? Do you have any marketing research or data on selling online?"

"One of our contacts did a case study on an online book seller called Amazon," Hank said. "They just went public on May fifteenth. Amazon has been highly successful as the leading online book retailer. Although they lose money, their yearly revenue growth is nearly three thousand percent. And Amazon's just selling books. Books? We'll be selling boats. As far as who we're targeting, Gordon, we're not going to begin with the entire country. We're not trying to boil the ocean, gents. I plan on piloting the website in only a few regions. A yacht dealer in Destin, Florida turned me on to that market. I'm looking at Eastern Nebraska, naturally. Then growing throughout Florida, starting with Destin and Pensacola, and then Lake Michigan as the initial pilot regions."

"I bet the commission on one yacht sale is significant," Todd said.

"Kaboom!" Hank animated an explosion with his hands and mouth, shaking his tie for the aftershock.

"It's a boatload," Gordon said, laughing at his own joke.

"So, how can we help you?" Todd asked.

"The marketing, fundraising, and general website functionality—well, you can leave that to me. I need help with the website design, development, hosting, and any other technical support. I'll want this to be online at 'I wanna buy a boat dot com' or something. I've registered a few domain names but haven't decided. I want you to demonstrate your competency in website development and, initially at a high level, show how the website might function and what the webpages would look like."

"I'm already thinking of design ideas as we speak," Robert said as he drew diagrams with his pen and notepad.

"See, look at that. Our CTO is already coming up with the architectural design."

"That's terrific, Todd. So, Todd's father turned me on to you young gents. And I trust Denny implicitly. Denny and I go way back." Hank smiled, as if awash in memories of all the good times he and Todd's father had shared throughout the years. "But I still want to see some specific ideas from you all, any comparable projects or case studies, and a brief pitch of your solution. Oh, and the commercials."

"Absolutely, we can do that," Gordon said.

This is bigger than anything we have done. I'm really not sure if we can do this. It may be out of reach—but is our best opportunity. Fake it until you make it.

"Just so you know, this is a competitive situation. I'm speaking to a few other Omaha consulting companies. But I do want to award this business to a partner where I can establish a long-term relationship. There'll be plenty of work ahead," Hank said.

"Could you tell us who they are?" Gordon asked, out on a limb.

"The competitors? No, I'm afraid we cannot disclose that," the lawyer said.

"Understood."

"Did I miss anything, Frank?" Hank asked the lawyer.

"Not at this juncture," Frank answered.

"Mr. Sherman, it was terrific to meet with you," Todd said.

"Yes, Mr. Sherman, thank you for giving us this opportunity," Gordon said.

"My pleasure. And you can call me Hank."

Hank and Frank, what a great pair.

They rotated stiffly around the conference room to work out each handshaking combination while trying to avoid intersecting. Hank Sherman handed out his business card to each of them. Gordon added Sagan Software business cards to their ever-growing list of to-dos.

"I'm capturing a list of screens that we'll need to create," Gordon said. He crouched down in front of the whiteboard in the basement and scrawled a list with the stinky dry-erase marker. "We'll have the home page, a menu, the registration form, a boat listing page, a boat view page, a help page, and an about the company page—"

"Wait guys," Robert said. "We've never developed anything like this before. Do we know what we're doing?"

"What do you mean, homie? I thought that's what we're doing right now?" Todd flicked his tongue ring.

"What I mean, Todd," Robert said, collecting his patience, "is do we know *how* this website will function? We've programmed only simple forms and static webpages—"

"Todd, would you please stop playing with your tongue ring," Vikram said.

"It's a stud and it's really none of your business," Todd said.

"It is *literally* our business, Todd. Do you think that looks very professional?" Robert asked.

"Fine, I'll take it out during customer meetings. Keep going with what were you saying, Robert."

"We've built a few trivial JavaScript functions. But this boat dealer site needs to be more dynamic, derived from a constantly changing boat listing database. How does it get updated? On the fly?"

"You can figure it out," Todd said dismissively. "You're the brains behind this operation."

"No, Robert is right," Vikram said. "This is uncharted waters for Sagan Software. I don't think we've ever done any websites that are this dynamic. I have been reading up on Apache, web servers, and CGI. Check out this magazine article. Truly cutting edge." Vikram tossed a magazine across the room and knocked over some empty beer cans.

"What are the scripts written in?" Gordon asked.

"Perl."

"I think I've seen this in action. Did you guys ever notice websites that have CGI-bin in the URL? They must be using it," Gordon said.

"That's right," Vikram said. "If we decide to build a prototype, I should be able to configure the Apache web server on our Linux box. Robert, do you think we're ready to code something?"

"I'm not sure yet. Does each webpage request fork off a new process on the web server to interpret the scripts and process the response?" Robert asked.

"Yes, as far as I understand it."

"And we'll be hosting this boat website from where? And on what server?"

Vikram, Todd, and Gordon pointed in unison toward their basement utility room.

"If Hank is throwing the kitchen sink at marketing, then we'll probably be getting a ton of hits on this boat site. You think our server can handle it?" Robert looked skeptical.

"I'm uncertain whether we'll have the processing power, not to mention the internet bandwidth. Let's not forget everything else running on the Aragorn server. Gandalf is overloaded too; I've been monitoring everything," Vikram said.

"Even if CGI is the future, I don't think Sagan Software is ready for a CGI project. It isn't just about bandwidth. I'm not confident I can program this on my own that quickly. I need to figure out something simpler for this prototype." Robert faced the whiteboard in deep contemplation and scratched his goatee.

"We have to do something about our workspace," Gordon said. "We've got two more full-time employees and have work for at least three interns now. But no office space. We can't have them in the basement. We've got several more website projects and Todd is going to close a couple more programming contracts."

"This basement is a crammed mess," Todd added.

Gordon tidied up the room, picked up dirty plates, and moved the bong to its rightful place.

"Can we even afford office space?" Robert asked.

"Let me work on that," Gordon said.

Vikram joined them for a caffeinated all-nighter design session at the whiteboard. Robert took charge of the design and laid out a brilliant plan to replace the CGI architecture.

"I'll write a script that reads from the database and writes out the HTML pages that need updating," he said, "such as the boats listing page and the boat detail page. The pages will be static as far as the web server is concerned, but they'll be updated periodically."

"Brilliant, Robert," Vikram said. "This is a highly scalable architecture. Scalability over consistency. I could set up a cron job on the Linux server to kick off the scripts nightly."

"Excellent work," Gordon said.

"How long would this take you to build Robert?" Todd asked.

"I already started working on it. I almost have a working proof of concept. I don't have any of the scheduling part, but I have written a script that reads the listing from the database and writes a simple HTML page."

"Okay. So, Vikram, you work on the scheduler. And Robert you can finish up the HTML prototype."

"Excellent job." Todd yawned. "I'm sure Hank and Frank will be impressed. Now let's get some sleep."

{-----}

Gordon sat in Gary's cluttered office, waiting, staring out the glass doors into the courtyard. Gary pecked at his keyboard and grunted at his computer monitor.

"So, do you watch cable TV?" Gary asked. He leaned back and swiveled in his chair.

Gordon shook his head. "Not often. I mean, sometimes. I've been very busy with work and school, and a social life."

"That *Home Improvement* show isn't bad. Tim Allen is a real funny guy. What really gets me, haha, that neighbor of his, Wilson? You know how they never let you see the rest of his face? That's so clever."

"Yeah, I've seen that show. It can be funny. It's a little too formulaic for my taste. He always gets in to trouble and then butchers some lesson to his wife that Wilson had taught him."

"Well, he's a Joe Everyman. You'll understand better someday when you're married and have kids. And have family values."

Didn't Tim Allen get busted for trafficking cocaine? He was in the game just like me.

"Do you have any children?" Gordon asked.

Gary laughed. "Oh, no way. Children are not for me. No pets either. Yes, it's a good show. That *Home Improvement*. At least they are not trying to push some liberal Hollywood agenda. Anyway, why'd you come over to talk about television, Gordon?"

"I didn't . . . Well, I came by to ask, uh, check in about the invoice. Did you happen to get that invoice?"

"I sure did."

"Were the hours and everything right?"

"It looked fine."

"I was just talking to Barbara about billing. She said she hadn't gotten anything in the mail from you."

"Well let's not get the banks and federal agencies involved in our little enterprise. You just deliver the invoices and I'll pay you directly in person. Wait here."

When Gary returned, he handed Gordon a stack of bills.

"Here's what I owe you. That should be enough."

"Cash? Oh, okay. That works too. We take checks as well, but cash works great." Gordon was elated.

"No, thank you. I'm moving toward all cash transactions. No banks involved. Didn't I tell you about the year 2000 problem? It's going to hit the banks worse. Plus, it really ticks my wife off when I don't trust the banks. I've got all my cash in a safe—well, never mind, I'm not telling you. You know, I'm stockpiling for the year 2000."

"Yes, I remember that," Gordon said uncomfortably.

"You guys should be thinking about the year 2000 problem too, especially in the tech world. Figure out what's going to happen while you have time."

Gary stood and grabbed his little rubber basketball, performed a pump fake, and hit a jumper from outside the file cabinet perimeter.

"Three!" he shouted. He stopped, listening. "I hear the garage door opening. I'm not in my office, I'm out in the shed working on the mower." He dodged out through the sliding doors to the courtyard.

With a pocketful of cash, Gordon let himself out the back courtyard too.

13/ LAUNDRY DAY

Summer 1997

It is the complex task that requires all of us to work together,
Every government agency, every university, every hospital,
Every business, large and small.

—President Bill Clinton

Barbara had left a message for Gordon on the house microcassette answering machine. Gordon was frustrated that she could never remember to call his cellular phone. He pressed the play button.

"Hello, Gordon. This is Barbara. I hope you are having a wonderful week. I have a question for you, umm, relating to accounts receivable. It may be easier to talk about it in person. I can discuss it with Todd instead, if you would prefer. Anyway, please just give me a call or stop by at your convenience. And have a wonderful day."

Gordon planned to return Barbara's message, but he also received a terse message from Dino on his cellular phone. Gordon called Dino back first.

"Hey Dino, I think I'm trained and ready for the next game at the Y."

"Good, man. How many points you think you'll score?"

"I'll put up twice as many points as last game."

"I'm a fan."

"Meet you down there this evening."

Gordon hung up and returned Barbara's call.

"Hi Barbara, I got your message. Remember, you can always call me on my cellular phone."

"Hello, Gordon, how are you doing today?"

"I'm fine, Barbara. This accounting thing, let me handle this on my own."

"Okay, Gordon. Did you want to come over and see me then? Or do you want me to just explain it now over the phone? It's about an overpayment."

"I'll meet you at your house to discuss. Are you free?"

"I'm available all afternoon, honey."

"I'm on my way."

Gordon sat at the dining room table and sipped ice-cold Rocky Top cola. He considered all his options. Perhaps an oatmeal cookie.

"So, I have this payment from Gary. It's in cash. Let me count it again." Barbara licked her fingers and counted the bills out in neat stacks.

"What's the issue with the payment?"

"It's an overpayment. Here's the account invoice."

"Oh, I see there's another invoice that is much higher. We have a fleet of interns working for him now at a good rate." Gordon wrote out a higher figure. "Now this should be right."

"Goodness, that's quite a windfall then," Barbara said, hand over heart. "You boys are doing some real nice business with Gary's account, aren't you?"

"Yeah, we are. That should be right, but let me get back with you on that," Gordon said.

"Speaking of windfalls, you wouldn't believe the weekend I had at an auction. Henry and I went to this estate sale and . . . Well, anyhow. Let me know as soon as you have the new invoice details and I can send that over to him."

"I'll call you tomorrow on that. I'll hand deliver all Gary's invoices moving forward. He just lives over by Todd Wallace's parents so it's not inconvenient."

"That's a nice neighborhood. Are you sure you don't want me just to ask Todd?" Barbara grabbed a Fig Newton and offered one up to Gordon.

"No, I'll take care of handling all Gary's invoices—and Fig Newtons—by myself," Gordon said.

Barbara started putting away the money and invoice files. "I don't mean to pry, but why is it that Gary wants to pay in cash?"

"Gary's a wing nut. He doesn't trust the banks, so he doesn't want to write checks. And he doesn't like the federal government either so doesn't want to send anything through the postal service."

"Well, I could speak with him if you'd like me to," Barbara offered.

"Thanks, but that's all right," Gordon said. That is one conversation he knew would not go over well.

{-----}

Gordon envisaged a land far from the Nebraska prairies where crashing waves, seagulls, and lighthouses substituted cornrows, barns, and windmills. He dreamt of an upscale coastal town in a northeast state, like Connecticut, that he had never visited. In a coastal village, a marina cove interspersed with shiny yachts and sailboats bobbing in the glistening waves. A cozy bar facing the docks, frequented by the locals who were all rich, young, and beautiful. Gordon dreamt of hobnobbing with his mates, leaning against the bar, wearing his yacht club sporting jacket with a nautical emblem. A surly stubbled sailor, an outsider, wobbling in from the docks and telling fantastic tales from the sea with his sharp, foreign accent. Gordon trying to one-up him with his own adventures, calling out his fables. All the patrons leaning in and encouraging them.

He was startled by the loud coughing fits outside his bedroom. Half awake, he clung to his dream state, covering his head with the comforter. Finally, he lumbered out to the couch to join Damian, who offered him a hit from the bong. *Smoke first, ask questions later.* Gordon exhaled, coughed, and glanced at the whiteboard filled with workflows, ER diagrams, and other designs that Robert had been working on for the boat website. Gordon had a fleeting concern that he wasn't going to be productive starting the day in this manner.

"Can I turn on some music?" Damian asked. Gordon nodded. "I've told you about my dream, Gordo. I'm going to make the perfect new drug."

"Like the Huey Lewis and the News song?"

"Yeah, pretty much. But first I want to figure out how to synthesize my own MDMA in a lab. Then I can make derivatives from there. I need to procure some precursors to MDMA. You know, MDMA is a methamphetamine, like crystal meth, but like mescaline too."

"I didn't know that," Gordon said. "You have a lab?"

Damian often became chatty during these wake-and-bake sessions while Gordon usually went taciturn. If he smoked too much in the morning, he was inclined to space out and spiral into introspection.

"You'll never guess what I need to make MDMA." Damian paused to light a cigarette. "Sassafras. If I can harvest some sassafras, then I can extract safrole to produce MDMA. Well, it's not quite that simple but, yeah."

"I'm not even sure what that is. Is that like the drink?"

"No, you're thinking of Sarsaparilla. Sassafras is an aromatic tree native to north and northeast America where it can be found in abundance. Its leaves and roots have medicinal value."

"How do you know all this stuff?"

"Gordo, I'm a chemist."

Gordon could not picture Damian as a real scientist in a lab coat as he watched him crawl on his hands and knees in his baggy clothes to put disc one of the Phish album *A Live One* into the CD player.

"More like an *alchemist* really," Damian said. "My dream, Gordo, needs to start small. I'm synthesizing the simpler and safer drugs. Then I'll go and harvest sassafras and set up my lab."

"You know I had a dream this morning about a northeastern sea village."

"Gordo, that is clairvoyance. Like the Iroquois Indians believed that dreams contained spiritual guidance. Your dreams are guiding us toward the Northeast."

Damian pressed play on the remote and they bounced around to the first Phish song.

"I want you to try something. It'll be fun," he said.

"What?" Gordon asked.

"This was easy to make." Damian pulled a tightly packed square of aluminum foil from his pocket and unfolded it. He took the Phish CD case and poured out some powder and made a line.

Gordon watched him closely. "What the hell is it?"

"Oh, and take this too." Damian handed him a pill. "You need to embrace new adventures in consciousness. Be a good psychonaut. I'll tell you what that pill is, Gordo. I bought it legally from the drugstore. It's 5HTP, a precursor to serotonin. You should buy some and take them regularly to build up your reserve, so you don't drain your brain on E."

Gordon swallowed the pill without water. Then he snorted a line with Damian Charlock, the alchemist, who watched him approvingly.

"Now, there's a good mind traveler."

14 / TONYA

Summer 1997

Love is a state in which a man sees things exactly as they are not.

—Friedrich Nietzsche

Gordon waited anxiously, pacing around the house with his phone. Though he was expecting a call from Hank, it was Tonya he was stressing out over. Worthless Brad from high school had come through and left Tonya's number on Gordon's answering machine. After nearly fifteen years of crushing infatuation, Gordon worked up the nerve to call her.

"Who is this?" she asked after she answered.

"It's Gordon."

Radio silence.

"Who?"

"Gordon Hamilton, from high school. Remember—"

"Oh. Okay, I haven't seen you in, like, forever. So, how'd you get my number?"

"Worthless Brad gave it to me."

"What are you calling for?"

Gordon hesitated and then took a deep breath and plunged ahead. "I just wanted to see if, well . . . if you wanted to go out some time."

"Go out where? Hehe, this is a surprise."

"Are you laughing?"

"No, maybe. I don't know. I just didn't expect you to call."

"There's a new restaurant that opened by the mall. Maybe we could go there together sometime?" Gordon suggested.

"D'you mean Chili's?" an older woman's voice asked.

"Mom!" Tonya shouted. "I told you I've got it. Get off the line!"

Gordon heard the *click* as Tonya's mother hung up.

"Is this your parent's house?" Gordon asked.

"Yeah, no duh. Like, what number did you think Worthless Brad would give you?"

"Why are you at your parents?"

"Because it's the weekend. And I like being home with my parents. Except when they eavesdrop on my calls, that is."

Gordon pictured her painting her toenails and twisting the spiral phone cord.

"Do you live there still?"

"No, I moved into an apartment. I have a roommate."

"You still haven't answered my question."

"Ask me again."

Is this flirting or just a fucking stupid conversation?

"Would you like to go to dinner with me?"

"I'll think about it."

"Can I call you back?"

"Call me later next week."

"Okay, I'll be thinking about you."

"Okay, Gordon. Bye."

{-----}

Hank and Frank looked intently across the table at Todd, Robert, and Gordon in the dimly lit conference room. The Sagan team had prepared a Power-Point presentation and live demo prototype but they needed to connect Todd's laptop to the room projector. Todd searched nervously in his bag.

"I can't find the right adapter," he said, sweating visibly from his upper lip and forehead.

Lights turning off and on, Hank shouting into the hall unintelligibly, IT guy coming in, trying a different dongle.

The law of demos.

I'm supposed to make small talk. Maybe talk about Warren Buffet's house in Omaha, that's just an ordinary ranch home.

"I have another meeting on the hour," Frank said, looking at his watch. Finally, someone arrived with the correct adapter and they were able to begin.

Gordon and Todd rushed through slides introducing themselves and an overview of Sagan Software before handing it over to Robert.

"This first slide is a simple diagram of our technical design," Robert said.

"It doesn't look simple to me," Hank said. "I'm not literate on technical schematics but I'll take your word for it."

"See, that job over there, that rectangle with the lines coming out of it, that updates the webpages from the database periodically," Robert explained.

"How often is periodically?"

"Well, that can be configured in the—"

"It's a setting. You can decide if it's every hour or nightly, up to you," Gordon clarified.

Frank looked at his watch again. "Can you show us the demo?"

"Sure, of course." Robert pulled up the browser and hit refresh.

An error screen displayed in the Netscape Navigator 4.0 browser.

Gordon's eyes widened. Todd drummed his fingertips on the table in a chaotic beat. Everyone looked at Robert.

"Oh, I'm sorry, let me see," he said, visibly shaking as he took a few deep breaths. "I'm sorry, this was working this morning."

"I need to go, gentlemen." Frank stood up. "I just want to say I appreciate all the effort and time you have put in, and wish you a promising future." He nodded to them and left the conference room.

"Please, relax," Hank said. "Don't apologize. I can spare a few more minutes." He leaned back and straightened his tie.

"Were you making changes to the boat listing page this morning? I told you not to make any more changes before the demo," Todd whispered to Robert.

"Yeah, you're right. Look—there it is. I must have fat fingered that HTML tag. I'm so sorry, I think I can still fix this." Robert took another deep breath. "I'm sorry. Oh, lookie there."

He refreshed the browser and a boat screen showed up. The new design had been improved with colorful 3D tables inside tables with brilliantly thick multi-color table borders. The Sagan team was proud of this modern design.

"Okay, now I'm scrolling down the screen and seeing the boat listings. Here . . . I can sort the boats by price or by date," Robert said.

"Very nice, gentlemen." Hank nodded approvingly. "This looks great."

Gordon felt he could cry with joy.

"Thank you, Hank," Robert said. "And there's more. So, say that I want to look more closely at one of the listed boats. If I just click here on the picture or link, then it opens a screen showing the boat details."

"I like it," Hank said. "Thanks a million. Again, gentlemen, great progress. I'm glad you sorted it out, Robert. We will be in touch." Hank stood and shook their hands before he left the conference room.

Gordon, Robert, and Todd exchanged high fives.

Stay confident. We can win this deal.

{-----}

"We were impressed by Sagan's progress and want to support you on your journey. I shared my positive feedback with Frank too," Hank Sherman said to Gordon over the phone a few days later.

"Thank you, Hank. So, are we in business?" Gordon asked from his place on the basement couch, watching muted cartoons with Damian.

"Well, not exactly. Gordon, we've decided to go in another direction. We need a more experienced partner for our investors. I had a great conversation with Denny Wallace, Todd's father, though, and I wanted to offer you, shall we say, a parting gift. I'm going to arrange a VC meeting, if you're interested. It's only a mentoring opportunity, not a pitch."

"VC. Okay, I'm interested, go on," Gordon said. He made a timeout gesture to Damian, who was reaching for the bong.

"VC as in venture capital. Financial firms that invest in startups and small businesses like yours. They can provide some great managerial advice and feedback on your business. I don't want to get your hopes up on funding, just a great learning experience and networking opportunity. I wouldn't pass on it if I were you."

"Yeah, of course. Well, sounds promising," Gordon said. "I'm definitely interested."

"I'll have my assistant follow up with the details."

"Thank you, Hank. I appreciate your consideration. Keep us in mind if you have anything else."

"Sure thing, Gordon. Stay in touch."

Click.

"What's going on?" Damian asked.

Gordon slumped back on the couch. "We didn't get the deal."

He got up and went upstairs, ignoring Damian's offer of the bong. As he approached the back door, a massive shadowy figure of a man loomed from outside. The damp hair, braided goatee, and size fifteen work boots could only be one person.

Not now, Dino.

15/ NEW YORK, NEW YORK

Fall 1997

Give me such shows—give me the streets of Manhattan!
—Walt Whitman

"Why did you bring such a big bag?" Robert asked Gordon as they waited at the baggage claim. "We are only staying for a few days."

"Are we in the city now? So far, I'm not impressed," Todd said.

"No, we're in the Newark airport. This is New Jersey. We're not even in New York yet. We just need to catch a train to Manhattan," Robert said.

"How the hell do you get to the trains?" Gordon knew how obvious it was that they were from out of town.

"I'll come with you to the train station, but that's where I'll bid you all a good day," Damian said.

Naturally, they chose Times Square as the first tourist site. Gordon located the iconic but comparatively small Coca Cola sign. Then Virgin, JVC, so many other signs and ads, rolling digital stock tickers, billboards for *Titanic*, *Good Will Hunting*, and other blockbuster movies, and *The Lion King* on Broadway, coming this fall.

"Yo, we should totally come down here for New Year's Eve," Todd said. Words never uttered by New York City businessmen who preferred not to freeze in two inches of slush, corralled like animals, resorting to public urination on building walls, just to witness a faint, distant bulb-covered ball slide down a short pole.

Yellow taxis honking, mobs of pedestrians shouting, hip hop music pouring out of a ghetto blaster. Whiffs of exhaust and cigarette smoke, hot dogs, Sbarro pizza, garbage, wafts of urine. PEEP LAND, nude shows, Live Girls Live. Boxed up windows.

At the Empire State Building, Gordon admired early twentieth-century gothic architecture, recalling his childhood watching *King Kong* in black and white in his cozy Nebraska basement. Wall Street, the mecca for businessmen, seemed small and crammed in the shadows, and Gordon was disappointingly unmoved. From the World Trade Center observation deck, he crawled between the vertical bars and leaned against the cold glass, peering out at the dizzying heights. He was up in the sky with the clouds, the tops of other skyscrapers far beneath him, the world curved, visible for miles. Tiny boats left trails in the brown water. The city sprawled beneath like a world to explore and conquer.

"That really messes with me, going out against the glass. I can't go out all the way," Robert said.

"Look how small the Statue of Liberty is," Todd said.

"Isn't it exhilarating doing business here the big city?!" Gordon exclaimed. He had never felt so alive walking through the city, as they headed back to the hotel before it was too late. They had a big day tomorrow.

Damian stepped off a bus outside of Philadelphia and unfolded his map. Hitchhiking from a truck stop, he headed westward, where rolling forested countryside replaced the city landscape. Damian bounced silently in the cab next to the taciturn truck driver, who uttered only one sentence: "Best come here in the fall when the leaves change." At the next junction, he met a young couple driving a pickup truck and agreed to ride in the bed with their dog. Damian knew they were hippies by the girl's sundress and their way of speaking, as if all flower children attended the same hippie grammar school. They passed Amish buggies trotting down paved streets and through winding wooded roads and one-lane bridges. They filled up at a gas station and Damian paid them a few dollars.

"Yeaahhhhh, man," she said. An answer to a question never asked. "Yeah, man. We have a place in the country with a vegetable garden. We mostly try to live off the land."

And, as it turned out, they lived mostly off her boyfriend's father, squatting in a trailer on his property. Damian arranged to pay the young couple a few more dollars if he could sleep on their property that night. He pitched a borrowed tent that evening, and just before sunset, they lit a bonfire. As they circled the fire, Damian thought of the Wednesday Night Sessions in Nebraska. He readily accepted an offer from the peace pipe.

"What brings you here to these parts?" the boyfriend asked.

"I'm gathering natural herbs and supplements," Damian said covertly, then realized who he was talking to. "I'm hunting for sassafras trees, among other things. I'll harvest oils and extracts from their roots, leaves, and bark."

"Right on. Don't they have leaves that grow into three-toed feet?" the girlfriend asked.

"Dude, I know where you can find those. Old Man Andersen's, just down the road. He has a pond and a large, wooded acreage," the boyfriend said.

"Great. I'll pack up in the morning and head that way."

"I dig your natural style, man," the girlfriend said. "The local Amish, now, they know how to live off the land better than us. Family farms are the only way, man, not factory farms. Industrial farming is taking over family farms in Nebraska?"

Damian gazed at her hairy legs stretching toward the crackling fire and said nothing.

"My father said it's hard to have a family farm anymore," the boyfriend added. "We're organic farmers. Small lot. We don't use products from Monsanto or big corporations or nothing, right sweetie pie?"

Damian was thinking only about his plans the next morning on Old Man Andersen's land. He was a psychonaut raver, not a tree hugger, and had never concerned himself with Nebraska farming. He had used their better nature for a ride, to squat on squatters, and harvest safrole. Damian noticed that they were freeloading off of capitalism and not contributing much with their idealism.

"Is the baby cryin' again?" the girlfriend asked.

{-----}

Robert and Gordon woke to find that Todd had already left the hotel room. Robert read a short note to Gordon: "*Had to run some errands. Will meet you at Corinthian Venture Partners. Todd.*"

"What errands would Todd have? What a flake!" Gordon said.

"Who cares, as long as he's on time. Are you wearing a tie too? Does this look straight?" Robert frowned at his reflection in the mirror.

When they arrived at the right building, they breezed past the front desk until security guards stopped them to sign in and wait for an escort. One could walk freely in and out of any office space in Lincoln, Nebraska.

"A bit much on the security around here," Robert said.

They were taken to a conference room with a full view of the gleaming steel and glass skyline. *We're high enough to look down at the roofs of other high rises. All right, be confident. Where should I sit? Just relax.* Gordon took several deep breaths until he was lightheaded. Robert placed the Sagan Software printouts around the table and left a stack in the middle.

Arthur Ravencrow arrived a few minutes later. "Hi, good morning, gentlemen. I'm Arthur Ravencrow. I'm a partner at Corinthian Ventures." He shook hands firmly with Robert and Gordon. Gordon gazed at Arthur's designer glasses, cufflinks, Rolex, custom tailored suit, and followed it down to his socks, and polished wing tip shoes. Gordon was instantly self-conscious about his cheap mall khakis, thick socks, and brown loafers.

Todd was the last one to enter the conference room and take a seat. An assistant served water from a carafe.

"Are we expecting anyone else? Or should we go ahead and get started?" Gordon asked.

"Let's get started. It'll probably just be me," Arthur said.

Robert and Gordon walked through their presentation, including an executive overview of Sagan and a review of their current book of business. Robert paused to ask Arthur if he had any questions.

"Hank Sherman and Denny Wallace, Todd's father, are both old friends of mine. They spoke highly of you, Gordon, and Sagan Software. I know you weren't expecting to pitch anything today, but I need to see some notion of a business plan."

"We were just getting ready to go over some new ideas," Gordon said.

"Ideas are easy. Ideas alone are worth next to nothing. Anyone can have a good idea but fail on execution. Furthermore, I don't invest in ideas alone, I invest in people. I do like you, Gordon. I like what I've heard about you. I like your passion and persistence, but you still need substance," Arthur said.

"First, I want to share our appreciation, Arthur. We are here for advisement, and we appreciate your time and attention."

"But you need some notion of a business plan. As an investor, I need to see growth from my investment," Arthur said. "What is your value proposition? What problem are you solving for your customers? Do you have a unique product or service offering? What is compelling about your company? How are you any different from your competition? Do you have some original intellectual property? Something of unique value?"

"We're working on an investment platform for a customer—"

"Okay, good. That's a start. So, is that your product, or your customer's product?"

"I see what you mean, Arthur," Robert said. "It is the customer's, sir," he added.

"I know you weren't prepared for a pitch and were only seeking advisement. Clearly, you're nowhere near ready. Take some time to develop before meeting with VCs for seed capital. If you need early investors—and this is common at your stage—look to friends and family members. Angel investors are also becoming more common. Not sure what's happening out in Lincoln. Check with your local chamber. Talk to their biz dev folks. See if there are any grant programs or startup groups."

"Great advice, Arthur. We haven't done all that yet," Gordon said.

"Listen, I've got to run," Arthur said. He stood up, buttoned his jacket, and walked toward the door. "I've arranged a small surprise for you all. You should celebrate what you've accomplished already. It takes more guts than most people have just to make it here. Keep it up. Diana will coordinate the rest for you."

"Thank you, Arthur."

"Enjoy the city, gentlemen. Cheers."

{-----}

Damian dug up several roots from the sassafras tree and placed them carefully in a plastic bag, with the leaves. His toes were cold from the morning dew, his breath visible. An old man took him by surprise, creep-ing through the deep forest in overalls and stalking cap. A dead ringer for Ernest Hemingway, who he presumed to be Old Man Andersen.

"What the hell are you doing on my property?" Andersen said gruffly.

"I was just taking a hike through the woods," Damian said.

"I saw you take something from my land. *My* land! And put it in that bag of yours. I saw you. Now hand it over to me you little son of a bitch," Andersen shouted.

Old Man Andersen pulled at Damian's backpack with surprising strength and almost knocked him over. Damian slipped out from the shoulder straps and yanked at the backpack with both arms.

"That is assault!" he shouted.

As soon as Damian was able to free it from the old man's grip, he hightailed it toward the trail that led to the highway, Andersen's shouts fading in the distance.

"You're trespassing, young man! Stay off my property! If I see you again, I'll take the law into my own hands. Don't tempt me!"

Damian hurried back to the young couple's trailer. Finding no sign of the them, he trekked to the highway to hitchhike back to the bus station.

{-----}

At a swanky downtown bar, Gordon approached the maître d and said, "Arthur Ravencrow made arrangements for us."

"Of course, gentlemen. Follow me," said the maître d.

They entered the large open room and were seated at a round table with leather club chairs, next to the grand fireplace. A waiter placed water glasses, complimentary snacks, and drink menus in front of them.

"Holy shit!" Robert exclaimed. "This one drink costs eight dollars. We could have *eight* drinks back home for that on dollar everything night."

"Or *thirty-two* draws on quarter draws night," Gordon added.

"We're not paying, so let's enjoy it. And don't embarrass us, Robert," Todd said.

Gordon peered above the tall fireplace at the painted fillagree on the high ceiling. A bartender in vest and bowtie rattled a cocktail shaker. Gordon felt like he had been transported into a better, grander life.

"We made some great connections today. Let's drink to my father for making all this possible," Todd said.

They clinked glasses.

"Let's drink to Arthur Ravencrow. And Sagan Software," Robert added.

"Let's drink to Gary," Gordon said. An idea was starting to form and take shape. "Arthur was right. We need to acquire Gary's product. It's mostly developed already too."

"We don't have that kind of cash."

"We don't have *any* cash."

"We could help him out somehow."

"Okay, enough about work. Let's celebrate."

After a few classy drinks, the young gentlemen loosened up and found their way to an old ale house dating back to the mid-1800s. The server slid a half-dozen beer mugs at a time across the worn table. Before long, round after round, they had made themselves at home and reverted to acting like young Nebraskans. They somehow found their way back to the hotel room, tried to order room service, passed out, slept in, woke up to watch cable TV, and eventually greeted Damian on his return. All in all, a successful trip, Gordon thought.

16/ HOMEGROWN I
Fall 1997

Two souls, alas, are dwelling in my breast,
And one is striving to forsake its brother.

—Johann Wolfgang von Goethe, *Faust*

"I said that I would like to examine one of the Beanie Babies. May I just check one, please, and see if they're authentic unopened toys?" Barbara asked. "Maybe, your friend can be a dear and translate that too."

She stood behind the waste station next to the large, hairy Russian man and his diminutive partner. The man turned to his partner and argued violently in Russian. Barbara took one step closer but kept her distance. The men smelled of vodka, turnips, and armpits.

"*Da*, the dolls are real. The truckload is to be yours. The matter is in the hat. I mean business. Do you mean business or no?" the little Russian asked.

"Yes, I do. I brought cash. It's safe in my car with my partner," Barbara said.

"Good, my boss is happy then. We don't want him to be angry," the little Russian said.

"Oh, heaven's no," Barbara said. "I have a special treat for him. Maybe this will cheer him up."

She took a piece of cake out of her oversized purse, pulled back the cling wrap, and presented it to him. The man grabbed a fistful of cake and shoved it into his mouth. He mumbled a few more choice words to his partner and licked his thick fingers.

The little Russian opened the back of the van for Barbara. She peered in and saw it was filled with black garbage bags. The little Russian shook one of the bags by the throat.

"Pay now. Then take dolls," the Russian boss said.

Barbara went back to her car and returned with the cash in her purse and handed it to the large Russian boss.

"Now, if you'll just follow us to my storage unit, you can help us unload," Barbara said, motioning like a steering wheel.

"*Pai-dyom.* Let's go," the Russian boss said.

The Russians jumped into the van and followed Barbara and her partner to the storage unit. Barbara unlocked the door and lifted it open. The van circled the lot and backed up. The large Russian boss walked up, scratched his belly, and belched.

His little partner opened the van door. Barbara leaned into the hot, stuffy darkness. The van smelled like a sweaty locker room covered in plastic. The little Russian reached into one of the bags and pulled out a few unopened Beanie Babies. She carefully inspected a sample of the bean-filled plushies, each individually wrapped and unopened. The Ty brand packaging and labels looked legitimate, all long-retired characters, but she sensed something was not on the level.

"Are you sure these are authentic, unopened, and untampered Beanie Babies? Do you have the originals that we discussed?" Barbara asked.

"*Nyet,*" the Russian boss said.

"He said, 'Yes', they are real," the little Russian said.

The two Russians began pitching the plastic bags into the storage unit. The large boss flung the bags across the unit, grunting. Barbara watched them slide and hit the back wall, stirring up paper and dust into the air.

"There's no big hurry, is there? Please be more careful. Jeepers," Barbara said. She lifted one bag herself and lumbered into the storage unit. She stood and caught her breath. Then she went to work tidying up the strewn bags into neat rows.

The Russian boss cursed and swung his arms in the air after tossing a hefty bag toward her.

"What did he say?" Barbara asked.

"He said that it is getting late, and he is very thirsty," the little Russian said.

Barbara brightened. "Oh, well guess what, I brought some cold pops in my car. Do you want something to drink?"

They exchanged words in Russian again and fell into laughter.

"Pops," the little Russian said, popping his lips. And they erupted with laughter again. The large Russian boss laughed himself into a fit of coughing. He cleared his throat and spit on the parking lot.

{-----}

Damian cleared the workbench in the basement utility room turned makeshift lab. Dirty laundry and buckets substituted for lab coats and test tubes. He pulled from his backpack the prize from Old Man Andersen's farm. He admired the dried root bark of the sassafras tree spread out across the workbench. He washed the roots in the utility sink and then scraped the bark off using a potato peeler and knife. He set out the bark scrapings to dry on the paper towels.

Damian's next task was extracting safrole oil, a precursor to MDMA. He had assumed that, with the right apparatus, that next step would be easy. They had planned to set up a steam distillery set for extracting the safrole oil from the roots. He was expecting Gordon home any time to come to the rescue and soon, he heard footsteps heading down the basement stairs.

"Let east meet west," Gordon said. "You go first."

"We're like the natives who used the bark of sassafras trees for healing and other rituals. My dude, lookie here. I've got the bark ready and drying out. How did you fare?" Damain asked.

"Well, thankfully, essential oils are gaining popularity in the US. All I had to do was start an essential oils offshoot of Sagan. Then I ordered a steam still from a supply company. It's in the back of my car," Gordon said.

"Essential oils, and beer, have been around since the ancient Egyptians. Just leave the rest to your alchemist, Gordo."

"Shall we get it out of the car and set it up?" Gordon asked.

"Let's go."

{-----}

"Where did you get all of that cash?" Barbara's husband Henry asked.

"What cash do you mean?"

"I found a bag of cash in the closet. There must have been thousands of dollars. I was looking for an old photo album, and there it was," Henry said.

Barbara shrugged. "I moved the photo albums to the spare bedroom closet."

"There's nothing at all but Beanie Babies from floor to ceiling."

"That's not entirely true," Barbara said. "I made a path. And I've cleared a few out."

Henry shifted from his place on the couch, wincing. "Now you know, Barb, what with my bad back, that I can't be crawling around in there and lifting. Thank God you got rid of some of them. Not that I can tell. I just can't account for what you see in them."

"Well, you have your Keno and lottery tickets. And the bowling balls that you don't ever use. I don't see you bowling in your health now, honey. We all have our vices," Barbara said.

"You're not trying to avoid my question, are you? Where'd you get all that cash and what's to come of it? You said we've lost our retirement savings. According to your accounting, we're just scraping by." Henry gave her a perplexed look. "And then I'm coming across piles of cash in the closet."

"Henry, not to worry dear. That money is for Sagan Software. It's a long story but one of our clients prefers to hand off cash payments. Gordon, the young man running the company, thinks the client does not trust banks for some reason. Anyhow, I've already deposited that cash."

"But what about us?"

"Well, you're right, we *are* living paycheck to paycheck. But I have every reason to believe it's going to get better. The Sagan boys are young, but they're going to do very well. The computer business is profitable, based on my accounting. And when they make money, so do we." Barbara grinned.

"What if I told you I have an idea for the cash?" Henry said.

"Let me put that green bean casserole in the oven and then I'm all ears."

{-----}

Another long silence. This phone call wasn't going as well as he had hoped.

"Hey, do you talk to anybody from the old Havelock neighborhood?" Gordon asked, desperately trying to find a topic Tonya might be interested in talking about. "Besides Worthless Brad?"

"No, not really, like, not after moving out for college. I still talk to Ashley a lot, but she's not from the old neighborhood."

"Do you remember when I used to bicycle around your neighborhood? I was trying to show off." Gordon smiled at the memory.

"Not really," Tonya said, sounding bored. "I remember riding bikes a lot. I loved my banana seat bike."

"I had a BMX bike, best thing in the world."

"Oh, I do remember that gang of boys riding around the neighborhood. We hated you guys—especially when the war games started."

He laughed, thrilled she was able to recall the memory. "Oh yes! I loved that. We'd go out in the woods and build forts and play war games. We started with soft air BB guns. Then we got real BB guns. Only one pump allowed."

"You guys were jerks," Tonya said. "Worthless Brad and his friends were shooting at me and some of the other girls."

"I would never do that."

"They shot a girl in the butt and in the neck."

"Oh, you heard about that?"

"Yeah. It was one of my friends."

"The parents put a stop to us after that. At least, from then on, we only played war games in the woods."

Static. Inhale.

"Look, I have to go now, Gordon," Tonya finally said.

"Can I call later, about that Chili's date?"

Pause. "Sure."

Gordon hung up the phone. *I should call O'Neill. O'Neill is always good council, maybe not for love advice, but business at least.*

"O'Neill, how's it going?"

"Living the dream, Gordon. Living the dream," O'Neill said, chuckling. "What's up?"

"I don't know who to trust. I don't know what's real. How do you know?" Gordon asked.

"Well, you're gonna have to give me more than that," O'Neill said.

"So, here's the working plan. Arthur Ravencrow, that's the big shot partner in the New York VC firm, said there's big money in owning a product with intellectual property value. And we've got nothing. So based on his advice, we're going to give away some programming hours to a client in exchange for equity in their company. And then I've branched out a couple new ventures with the company. They're super high-risk. Moonshots." Gordon exhaled. "I don't know what I'm doing."

"One thing I've learned is that most people, even the most successful, don't know what they're doing or the risk they are taking. Otherwise, they wouldn't have gone for it in the first place. That's why you don't see middle-aged geezers like me going out on a limb. Gordon, it's what I admire you for."

"Yeah, but I'm taking a lot of risks. Scary risk."

"Like what do you mean? Talk to me about it."

As much as he wanted to disclose to someone exactly what he was involved in, Gordon knew he couldn't. "Actually, I'm not sure that I can."

"That doesn't sound good," O'Neill said. "Follow your heart, but more importantly, follow your moral compass. I know you know right from wrong. What choices you make, you live with forever."

"Are you speaking from experience?"

"Yes. But, heck, Gordon, I'm so very conservative. I've never taken big risks. I've seen others make mistakes they regret forever. Plus, I know those VC fat cats are only looking out for themselves. If they're funding you, they'll want something in return, or they'll eat you up and spit you out. You're disposable to them."

17/ HOMEGROWN II
Fall 1997

Come and trip as ye go,
On the light fantastic toe.

—John Milton

Gordon's chest was tight with anticipation for the Lincoln rave. His mind was racing. *I'm not an extraordinary person. I don't have the right stuff. Just a dumbshit from Nebraska. But look at me now, a CEO, doing business in NYC.*

But am I even a real CEO? The more easily achievable something is, the less legitimate it feels. The easiest way to become a CEO is to start a company and name yourself CEO. I started at the top of Sagan and have never been promoted once through merit. Meanwhile, I'm selling Dino's wares to other small-time dealers, climbing the rungs of a career ladder I never wanted. My goal was to work hard and play hard. Be successful. Rise above my situation and stand on the shoulders of others. Well, who's standing on my shoulders? An angel on one shoulder and a devil on the other.

Gordon followed a path toward the loud beats around the pine row to the farmhouse where a DJ was spinning electro beats from the front porch. Partiers filled the patio and porch swings. They headed toward the prairie pasture where three more DJs performed for dancing ravers. As the daylight faded, neon glowsticks and flashing lights bounced across a dark field. They transitioned from one DJ stage to another, the music clashing like Nashville's Broadway strip on speed.

"Hey, did you see who's up there?" Robert shouted excitedly over the music.

"Who?" Jennifer asked.

"My old roommate, Michael. Remember?"

Gordon remembered him playing music in Robert's dorm room and out at the Range. "That's right! What a perfect gig for him."

"One of your boys made it, Rob!" Jennifer said. "That's exciting."

Robert and Jennifer jumped and waved to get his attention. Michael pumped a fist toward them in time to the heavy beat while clinching his headphones between his ear and shoulder.

"Are Todd and Vikram coming? Where is Oliver?" Jennifer asked.

"Todd's not part of this world," Gordon said. "Neither is Vikram. Or Stuart. It's like George Constanza on *Seinfeld*. We can't have those two worlds colliding. Are we going to party or what?" He pulled out several new capsules of ecstasy and handed them out. "This one is on the house."

They moved to the main stage and, as Gordon lost track of time, the MDMA set in. His vision tunneled. His hair was cool and sweaty, legs wobbly, heart throbbing. A new track dropped, and he broke through on the other side with intense crystalized energy, his body mindlessly jumping up and down in tandem with Robert, Jennifer, Damian, and Debbie. The music had a direct circuit to his brain. He wasn't just listening to it, he was *feeling* it. And then he was *inside* of the music.

Debbie danced in her tracksuit decorated with glow-in-the-dark colors as she chewed on her pacifier. Gordon gazed at the neon tracers following her movements. He looked all around as he gathered his bearings. Across the matted, grassy dancefloor a tall, nice-looking black man, wearing a backward visor, danced with a stocky young man with dirty blond hair.

Gordon squinted, watching them. *Either I'm high or I'm seeing Oliver or both. It must be him. What are the odds?*

"It's Frodo, come on!" Gordon said, pulling Robert by the arm.

Oliver stopped like a deer in headlights.

"Frodo! Oliver, it's me, Gordon. Robert's here, too!"

"Wow," Oliver said, his eyes wide as he looked from Gordon to Robert. "I can't hide from it anymore. You found me out. We're not out in the open yet, so please."

Gordon looked at him quizzically. "Found what out? Found you? We sure did!"

"Found *us* out." Oliver looked at the guy he'd been dancing with. "This is Terrence. He's my partner . . . My boyfriend."

"This is awesome!" Gordon shouted. He was thrilled. "We should enjoy this moment together. I can't believe you guys like to go to raves too?!"

"Great to meet you finally," Robert said, holding his hand out.

Terrence shook hands with Robert and Gordon. "We go to raves almost every weekend."

"I'm surprised we haven't run into you before or like, why you didn't mention it before at the house. Are you rolling?" Gordon asked.

"Just look into my eyes," Terrence said.

"You're not upset with me, are you?" Oliver asked. "I kept it a secret because I didn't know."

"Of course not. We love you both!" Robert cried joyously.

They all embraced in a long group hug. Gordon felt such a sense of oneness with them as if everything was interconnected by something. Perhaps love. He was thrilled Oliver had found someone. Everyone deserved to be happy.

They went back to dancing and Gordon took in all the beautiful sights and sounds. A raver entertained them with a spinning contraption that drew words with LED lights in the air: "ARE YOU ROLLING?" Gordon's attention was pulled beyond the main stage where people seemed to be flocking in one direction. He looked the other way and was surprised by an array of different colorful blinking lights. These lights were on top of cars.

Shit, the police. This party is getting busted.

He shoved his way through the crowd, looking for his friends.

"We need to leave," he said when he finally found them. "Now! Police are here. And I'm holding."

"How much?" Robert asked.

"Too much. Enough to end everything," Gordon said.

"Walk back toward that wooded area and wait," Damian said. "I've got to find my other friend but then we'll come find you."

They marched to the edge of the field and into the woods. Gordon felt cold, as if the cold air was draining his high. Debbie, glowing like a beacon, offered him a cigarette, which he took in hopes it would help him chill. Oliver and Terrence huddled with their arms around each other.

Damian finally found them and they followed him down a trail through a cleared path covered in pine needles. The air was cool and piney fresh. After they had helped each other down the path, Damian turned on a tiny flashlight to illuminate the way. Gordon wanted to run but knew it wouldn't be safe. His mind was imagining things to fill the darkness, so he couldn't even be sure what was real. They piled into a car and shuttled down a country road toward a house outside the city. As they drove away safely, the mood rebounded, and they were chattering and laughing again. A small crowd quickly gathered in the little house, the music was on, and the party was back in full swing.

The living room was lit only with black lights and glowsticks. Gordon, the sole supplier of the house party, was in high demand. He dug through his cargo pockets, left side, right side, rolling, back pocket, deep breath, frantically doling out and counting money.

Robert's old roommate Michael had found his way to the house party, and it wasn't long before he was doing what he always wanted to do: DJ parties, make people happy, and get lost in the music. He shuffled through burned CDs of live DJ sets. Requests blurted out: Paul Oakenfold, Carl Cox, Sasha, John Digweed, Pete Tong. Michael filtered through popular suggestions and put in a rare live mix from Frankie Bones. The Brooklyn DJ brought the house down with raw caffeinated house beats. The jumping and dancing shook the floor, causing the CD to skip occasionally, only to resume with cheers and whistles.

Gordon, Damian, and Debbie took a break from dancing as they began coming down and retreated to the front porch for a smoke break.

"Isn't it just incredible how everything is interconnected?" Debbie exhaled a plume of smoke. "Like us and trees. The air we exhale . . . the um, carbon monoxide is what the trees breathe in. And the trees, in turn, create oxygen for us to breathe."

"I've been thinking the same thing all night," Gordon said. He made a feeble attempt to examine the trees in the front yard, but it was too dark.

"You know, Gordo," Damian said, "like Debbie says, everything is connected. E connects us together as humans. Yet E is a human creation and not entirely natural. Ecstasy was created in a lab by drug scientists. We want to fully connect with nature. I want to bring us closer to earth. And Debbie had the most terrific idea. Tell Gordon, Debbie, that there's a fungus among us."

Debbie grinned. "There is, Gordon, yes."

"Tell me more," he said.

"Fungi are their own unique kingdom of creatures, you know," she said.

"They're neither plant nor animal," Damian added. "Yet they're essential to all life forms on the planet. Integral to plants and animals. They create what's called a . . . uh, mycorrhizal network, forming their connection to the earth, plants, and animals."

"That's wild," Gordon said. "I didn't know that. I'd never thought of it like that before."

"Gordo, you'll dig this: A fungal network is like the world wide web."

Gordon envisaged a vast network under the soil, between roots, trees, and decomposing organic matter.

"Gordo, with your help, we can interconnect party people with nature. And create a new drug—no, a new culture—by combining these so-called designer drugs with traditional psychoactive chemicals found in mushrooms."

Pharma and farm.

"Like, you know, magic mushrooms," Debbie said.

Two strangers joined their smoking circle on the porch. The conversation changed from drugs to music, to the awesome rave and to the disturbing police bust, then back to music.

Just before sunrise, the remaining crew found a respite in the back sunroom, sprawling on sofas. They coupled as Damian and Debbie; Robert and Jennifer; Oliver and Terrence; and Michael with a new girlfriend. Gordon, by process of elimination, had paired with a young lady he assumed was from money and had gone to a private Catholic school. She wore a fashionable track suit, had straight hair and healthy tan skin. He never knew her name. Gordon wrapped his arms around her comfortable clothes, clinging and sweating. She leaned into him and released her tension. They had a special but ephemeral moment. Michael fired up a hookah and they passed it around, but Gordon did not partake.

Pharma and farm. Farm and pharma.

The party broke down into scattered conversation as the dawn's glow began to peek into the sunroom. Ambient drum and bass played from the living room. Gordon felt this weird sinking feeling in the pit of his stomach and downward. An awkward fluttering of humiliation and longing. He thought about Tonya and his wish that they would truly be together. His mind raced geometrically. Maybe he was trying to fill a void, some sort of painful yearning. He was grasping for something beyond his reach, and all this partying and risky behavior could not bring him solace.

Gordon walked the girl to her ride without sharing a word or making eye contact in the light of day. And he felt emptiness.

{-----}

Robert and Oliver had both already moved out due to irreconcilable differences. Robert had gotten fed up with the ferret and was not alone in blaming the varmint on a flea infestation. Oliver in turn complained about the curry and syrup smells emanating up into his room from the kitchen. Damian officially moved in upstairs, and Gordon made a permanent home in the basement. After their server outage, Vikram complained about Damain's experiment in the basement utility room, so Damian moved his equipment out of the house. It was all for the better and everyone remained friends.

As the gang surrounded a warm fire in the backyard, the Ford Galaxie approached with the unmistakable thundering engine and heavy gravel-crunching tires.

"Who on earth is that?" Terrence asked Oliver.

Gordon jumped in Dino's car for a short ride.

"I can trust you, can't I?" Dino said. He gave Gordon a grave look. "We're not under the radar anymore. Heat is the word on the street. Heat. Gordon. Can I trust you?"

Gordon looked out the Ford Galaxie's windshield.

"You know I'm legit," Gordon said. "Hell, I'm a CEO of a software company. I work hard every day."

"I don't know how you can do that complicated stuff *and* all this partying on E." Dino shook his head. "You know, I wanted to be an architectural engineer. I made it to my junior year before dropping out. My father was—well, my father *is*—a successful architect. And I've thrown that all away."

"I had no idea," Gordon said. "I've always thought highly of you, Dino. I know we're not best friends or anything, but we respect each other. We're in this together, man."

"I deal with all kinds of trash these days. The kind of people that I should never have associated with. I could take you to some sketchy part of Omaha and show you . . . But I won't. Just be careful around the kinds of people who have nothing to lose. You have a lot more to lose now."

"Don't worry, Dino. Trust me, man, you've got nothing to worry about with me."

"I hope so. I've just had a feeling, maybe it's nothing. We all need to be careful."

"Your real name isn't Dino, is it? If you trust me, you can tell me."

"Nah. Just be careful out there. Here's your rolls." Dino gave him four pill bottles. Gordon thanked him, hoping whatever feeling Dino had been having was wrong.

18/ INTELLECTUAL PROPRIETY

Winter 1997–98

Failure to achieve compliance with Year 2000 will jeopardize our way of living on this planet.

—Arthur Gross, CIO at the IRS

"We're here to talk to you about modernizing your program into a web application," Gordon said. He had rehearsed this line, making sure not to say "productize."

The Sagan team sat in Gary's elegant dining room, as Gary looked from Gordon, to Todd, to Robert, and then back to Gordon.

"Is that within my budget? Or are you trying to upsell me?" he asked.

"Let's not talk about the cost yet," Todd suggested. "Let's keep our eye on the potential."

Gary scoffed. "Easy for you to say."

"We can refactor the product to bring all the functionality of your Visual Basic application into a web application," Gordon said. "Then, as a web application, your program will be accessible to anyone on the internet through a web browser; password protected, of course. At Sagan, we've been working with a new technology stack to build true web applications."

"Using Java, Servlets, HTML, and JavaScript," Robert added.

"You mean a complete rewrite? You want to make it a website instead?"

Robert nodded. "Yes, it would be a rewrite on the UI, but we can leverage a lot of the existing backend code and business logic. The database won't need to change much."

"Gary, this is *cutting edge*." Todd splayed his hands on the table and leaned forward. "We're not building websites, but web *applications*. Sagan is leapfrogging over CGI to the forefront of technology with enterprise Java."

Gary smiled and leaned back in his chair. Gordon had hoped the word "enterprise" resonated.

"This is all powered by what are called Servlets. The Java Servlet Development Kit 1.0 was just released this June." Robert opened a browser with a website that showed a table of stocks and funds. "This list of data is coming directly from a database. Here, I'll click on one of the stocks." He paused, waiting for the page to refresh. "Now you can see it has queried the database and reloaded the page with the details of the stock. Inside the web browser!"

"Color me impressed," Gary said.

"But that's not it," Todd said with a surreptitious flick of the tongue stud. "Show him the menu icons and the folders."

"Yes, so look at this, Gary. I'm opening this folder icon, and then it expands and opens. It refreshes the entire page with the contents of that folder," Robert said.

Gary raised his eyebrows and nodded approvingly. "It looks like Windows 97, but inside a web browser! That is really slick. But what if it's just a fad? What you guys should really be getting into is solving this year 2000 problem."

"Funny you should mention it. We just kicked off a couple Y2K gigs," Gordon said.

"And I'm launching a new Y2K sales campaign next quarter," Todd added.

WE are launching, not just you, Todd.

"I told you it could spell doomsday. Don't come knocking on my door. Imagine if the banks close their doors, or if the power plants shut down, or heck, airplanes are falling from the sky," Gary mused. "So, tell me, what is the damage? To build this new website?"

"Web *application*," Robert corrected.

"Okee. Fine. Web *application*. What are you trying to charge me?"

"Nothing." Gordon shook his head. "We just want equity in the business."

"Equity? You mean part ownership?" Gary asked rhetorically. He blinked twice and spun around in his chair. "All right. I'll listen to an offer, but I'll still want controlling interest."

"We'll come back with an offer," Robert said.

"Okie-dokie. If that's the case, then, I'll walk you guys out." They stood up, following Gary toward the front door.

"That Clinton," Gary said as they stepped outside, "he's awful smooth, but I tell you, he's running around. That Slick Willie's a philanderer if I ever saw one. Just like JFK. All those Democrats with their virtuous talk about caring for the people. But time and time again, getting caught with their pants down. Democrats with loose morals and their—"

"See you later, Gary," Gordon said.

{-----}

Tonya was noncommittal about going out to dinner, so Gordon was willing to settle for a walk in the park to start. She wanted to take things slowly, and he would respect that—he was thrilled they were finally getting to spend a little bit of time together. He wanted to hold her hand but he couldn't work up the nerve yet to do it.

"Look at this cute pond," Tonya said. They stopped at the water's edge and watched the ducks drifting along the surface.

Gordon reached for her hand. If he kept thinking about it, he would never do it. It felt strange, but good, to feel her fingers intertwining with his own. For a moment, her hand felt limp in his but then she squeezed his hand lightly and didn't let go.

"Look at the mallards," Tonya said. "I love how their feathers shine in the sun, greens and the blues."

"Yeah, it's beautiful," Gordon said, looking at her as she kept her gaze on the ducks.

"We should probably get going," Tonya said after a minute. "I've got soccer practice soon. Our next game is on Thursday, did you want to go?"

Gordon gritted his teeth and forced a smile. He'd be happy watching her write a grocery list, but soccer was really not his thing. "So long as I don't have a work meeting, that sounds great. And hey, do you want to try to go to Chili's this Saturday? Are you free that evening?" He wanted to sit somewhere with her, just the two of them, with no soccer practice, no work commitments, getting in the way.

"Hmm, Saturday," Tonya said. "Yeah, I think we could do that." She grinned. "If you come to my game, that is."

"There's no place else I'd rather be," he said.

{-----}

After another cruise down O Street, Gordon drove to the Gateway Mall and parked outside Montgomery Wards. He was there to meet Damian, who he found in the food court, buying a soft pretzel.

"Let's go to Aladdin's Castle," Damian said. "I want to play some Skee-Ball."

"Thanks for meeting me somewhere public," Gordon said.

"It's all good. My new product is going to be ready soon. The essential oil extraction apparatus worked swimmingly. Dude, it's real close to completion."

Farm and pharma. Pharma and farm.

"The mill? Already ready? How is that possible?" Gordon asked.

"I've been working on it tirelessly day and night for weeks and weeks. I've dedicated my time to nothing else."

As in, he doesn't have a job and I doubt he attends class. Well, as long as he is paying rent and producing goods.

"Tell me what you've cooked up."

Damian took another bite of his pretzel. "So, I'm going for the super high energy feel good of E without too hard of a whack out. Crystal clear high, like you can jump through walls. Then a strong rollout with a fine earthy psychedelic finish."

They pushed coins in the slots, and the heavy wood balls rolled down the side pockets. Damian and Gordon tossed balls down the shoot, off the ramp, and into the white rings. Damian scored 50 right up the middle but Gordon threw his too hard at a 100 and it bounced down into the 10.

"Should we let Dino know?" Damian asked. "Is he in with us?"

"Of course we will. Dino has the first right of refusal. He's just another distributor, and we're supply and R&D. I'll keep my turf and we'll grow beyond his imagination. Dino is not as optimistic about our product ideas, but we can come to an agreement," Gordon said. He thought about his last conversation with Dino, and Dino's "feeling" that something could go awry. He was just being paranoid, Gordon had decided, and so he didn't feel the need to mention it now.

"You've talked to Dino about this? I just want to make sure there's no bad blood." Damian tossed a ball and scored another 50 points.

"Dino will be working for us on this project, not the other way around," Gordon said.

"I dig it. Okay, now for the fun question—"

Some young boys approached their lane. A menacing little curly-haired boy with braces asked, "Are you gonna hog this lane all day?"

"Not long. Go shoot hoops or something. Back off and give us some space," Gordon said.

Damian scowled at them. "Little punks."

"Forget them. That was us just a few years ago. Just need to be put in their place. So, what was your fun question?"

"We're finally getting to the question of the day." He leaned in close to Gordon so he could whisper. "What do you want us to press on them? How do you want to label the pills?"

"Oh, ah. I see. But the best rolls I've sold were always capsule—" Gordon stopped, looked around at the children playing arcades, whack-a-mole, hoops. He lowered his voice. "I've always sold capsules with powder."

"Think about the marketing opportunity, Gordo. Your new brand name. You want people asking for them by name, know what I'm sayin'?"

The entrepreneur inside Gordon understood. They rolled a few more times. Damian tore off a long ring of tickets to trade in for a garbage prize. They decided to go in on something together.

"Y2K!" Gordon said suddenly.

"Ah, what? Oh, you mean for the pills, right! Like, as in the year 2000 thingy? I like it. Short and catchy. I was hoping it was something short cause they're not very wide across."

"Y2K."

"You have a color preference? I can add some food coloring or something."

"Is food coloring healthy?"

"Ha."

"Blue. Baby blue."

"Groovy, Gordo." Damian grinned. "Consider it done."

19/ INTELLECTUAL PROPRIETY II

Winter 1997 – 98

What's going to happen when whole countries drop off the radar screen with no infrastructure remaining?

—Senator Bob Bennett (R-Utah), Chairman, Senate Special Committee on the Year 2000 Technology Problem

Tonya changed plans at the last minute and told Gordon she would meet him at Chili's, instead of having him pick her up. He was too anxiously excited to think much of it; he'd gone to her soccer game a few days ago, had suffered through the entire thing, and though he hadn't been invited to go out and celebrate with the team after their victory, he had at least managed to give Tonya a hug and re-confirm their date this weekend. Now, as he crossed the parking lot toward her, he saw that she was not alone.

"Oh, hey," Tonya said as Gordon tried to hide his surprise. "So, this is my best friend, Ashley. I totally got my weekends mixed up, I thought Ash was going to be visiting *next* weekend. But she's here now, and she wanted to meet you after everything I've told her about you, so I figured it'd be okay if she joined us. Is that okay, Gordon?" Tonya looked at him imploringly, her eyes wide.

"Yeah, it's no problem. The more the merrier," Gordon said.

This was supposed to be a date. Why the third wheel?

The three of them went inside and were led to a booth by the hostess. "So, where are you visiting from?" Gordon asked as they opened their menus.

"I drove up from Kansas," Ashley said. "I go to KU. The Jayhawks *not* the Wildcats."

Gordon smiled. "I know. I don't think we've met. Are you from Havelock or did you go to high school with us?"

"No. She moved away after sixth grade but we're still like best friends. I guess you don't remember her," Tonya said.

"You're twenty-one, aren't you, Gordon? Can you please, please order us drinks?" Ashley asked.

"Of course, he can, duh. Don't act suspicious." Tonya nudged her with her elbow and they both dissolved into giggles.

"So, are we going shopping after this?" Tonya asked.

"I would love to go shopping!" Ashley exclaimed. She looked across the table at Gordon. "Can you take us shopping? Don't you, like, have your own company or something? That's what Tonya was saying."

A shopping spree had not been on his agenda, but he was pleased to hear that Tonya had talked about him. "Yes, I have a software company. We offer bespoke software solutions and services for—"

"Would you to order me a Long Island Iced Tea?" Ashley asked.

"Well, I can get one for myself and share it but after that it's going to be weird. I guess I don't have to drink."

"You're driving, aren't you? That's probably a good idea then," Tonya said.

Ashley pushed a menu in front of her face, pointing. "Look at this! Can we get steaks? What is a Steak Pico? I love a good steak. Let's order them."

After the waiter took their order, Gordon sat back in the booth and watched as Tonya and Ashley whispered and giggled together, as if he weren't even there.

"You're not talking about me, are you?" Gordon asked in what he hoped was a friendly, joking tone.

"I promise you that we are *not* talking about you," Ashley said.

"Okay, just making sure. So, I was wondering: what kind of music are you interested in? Do you like electronic music?"

Tonya scoffed. "No."

"We like country music," Ashley said. She and Tonya turned their attention back to each other. Gordon sighed.

When their food arrived, he watched in amazement as the two girls laid siege to their meals. They were finished and requesting more drinks before he was even halfway done, though he wasn't feeling much of an appetite at this point anyway.

He paid the bill when it came, and they went back out to the parking lot.

"Gordon could you please, *please* take us to visit an old friend of ours? It'll be super quick. And then we can go out to our favorite club. I can't drive because I've had a few drinks."

"C'mon, Gordon, be a dear and drive us to the sorority." Tonya pulled on his arm and gave him a wide-eyed, pleading look.

"Sure, okay," he finally relented.

The two girls climbed into the backseat. "It's the Gamma Phi Beta sorority house," Ashley said. "I'll tell you where to go. We're going to go upstairs and visit her for just a sec. Boys aren't allowed in sorority rooms, so you'll have to wait, but we won't be long."

Gordon said nothing; it didn't seem that his presence, beyond being a sober chauffeur, was required. He testily skipped tracks on the CD player as he drove.

When they arrived, he wrote his cell phone number on the back of a receipt and gave it to Tonya. "Give me a call when you're ready," he said.

Tonya looked at him quizzically as she took it. "You're not going to wait? We won't be long."

"Just in case," he said.

He waited in the car, flipping through his CD case. After about thirty minutes, he realized that they may not be coming soon, and that he had no way of contacting them.

He finally gave up and drove back to his house. He put on a movie on to distract himself from the fact the "date" had gone nothing at all like what he'd hoped, not even close. Part of him said that he should just forget about her, move on. But there was another part of him that didn't want to give up yet. *She's just distracted cause her friend is in town.*

His cell phone rang about an hour into the movie. He picked it up, heard muffled conversation and loud music in the background.

"Hey, Gordon! It's Ashley, can you come pick us up at the club? Hold on—shut up everyone! I'm trying to talk to Gordon! What? No not him. Like, Gordon. Gordon, our ride—"

"I can barely hear you," Gordon said. "Can you put Tonya on?"

"She's busy now. Can you come get us? *Please?* It would mean a lot to us. Especially Tonya. She'll be so happy you came back to get us. I don't even know if we have a ride back to my car!"

Gordon sighed. She had to tell him twice what club they were at because it was so loud that he couldn't hear her. "Okay, I'll be there in ten minutes. Wait outside for me."

When he arrived, the two girls piled in the back again, laughing, barely paying him any attention. They wanted him to stop and pick up some beer, but he said no, despite their begging and pouty admonishments.

"Don't be lame, Gordon," Ashley said. "Tonya was telling me that you were cool. But this isn't being cool."

He glanced at her in his rearview mirror. "Are we ready?"

Ashley smirked, held his gaze. "Are you going to stop being so lame?"

Instead of directing him to Tonya's apartment, they gave him the address of a party Gordon had no interest in attending, though he was pretty sure he wasn't invited anyway.

"How are you getting back home to your apartment?" Gordon asked as they spilled out of the car. He looked at Ashley. "How are you getting your car?"

"I have a friend I can call," Tonya said. She leaned through the open driver's side window and kissed Gordon on the cheek. When she straightened, she and Ashley burst into laughter.

At home, Gordon tried to forget everything that happened before the kiss. But he could not. He felt ill. He tossed and turned in bed, going over each minute play by play, like a football coach after a crushing defeat.

Steve Jobs did not have anything on Damian's Y2K reveal in the basement utility room. The workbench was their center stage, lit with a bare seventy-five-watt lightbulb amidst an ambience of wet socks and mildew. Damian opened his backpack and pulled out giant orange pill bottles from the first batch.

"Have a look," he said, handing around a sampling of the blue Y2K branded tablets.

Dino maneuvered his head between the rafters. "So, have you tested these? Are they the bomb shit?"

"Oh yeah," Damian said. "I even tested a sample at a private rave party last weekend. Epic."

Gordon inspected one of the pills. "Dino, we know this will change our relationship. But you're still in charge of regional distribution. Damian is taking charge of manufacturing, but we'll give you first dibs on distribution in the Midwest."

This is some real gangster type shit. Except I'm not going to make Dino kiss my ring or anything.

Dino shook Gordon's hand, pulled him in and wrapped his arms around him, whispering in his ear, "You the man now Gordo, but don't ever screw me."

"You've got my word," Gordon said. When Dino released his hand, he looked over at Damian. "All right, time to ramp up production at the factory. As you know, I'm going to be delegating a lot of this because I have a software company to run. And you both know why that cover is a good thing."

And so it began. Y2K took off like gangbusters, quickly spreading across the Midwest and Central Plains. Dino already had a large network that extended beyond Gordon's expectations. Before long, Damian's prediction was correct, and people were asking for Y2K by name at raves and clubs from Fargo to Dallas.

A spacious house, creaking and reeking of old age, served as the new Sagan office space. It was like a twisted '90s version of *Upstairs, Downstairs*, where interns worked and partied in the basement, while the upstairs floors held private offices and conference rooms.

In his bedroom-turned-office, Gordon sat and admired his newly framed poster. No more Jack Parsons. He'd been replaced by the "Traitorous Eight", a 1960 black and white photo of the founders of Fairchild Semiconductor. Gordon's new hero, Robert Noyce, front and center, turning toward the camera, smiling with unwavering confidence. Noyce, who grew up in neighboring rural Iowa and once got suspended from college for stealing the mayor's pig for a college luau roast, went on to lead an illustrious career by inventing the integrated circuit, co-founding Intel, and becoming the de facto "Mayor of Silicon Valley." *Bob Noyce's inventions made all modern computing possible. He changed the entire world.*

"How do you think the meeting with Gary went?" Gordon asked at the start of the leadership meeting with Robert and Todd.

"I think it went well. We probably have a great chance of investing in his venture," Robert said.

"I agree. Gary seems motivated. You think it'll be our own dot com success some day?"

"Well, it's one iron in the fire," Robert said. Gordon looked at Todd, who was uncharacteristically quiet. He had just bleached and spiked his hair, which Gordon found irritating, though he couldn't say why.

"So, anyway, some quick announcements," Gordon said, looking down at the notepad in front of him. "Vikram is going full time. We can invite him to these meetings on a 'need' basis. The web designer is part time, for now. We have an ad for more interns and both full-time and part-time programmers. Robert, leverage your connections with the professors at UNL. We'll need plenty of help for these new Y2K projects. Speaking of, how is the new sales campaign, Todd?"

"The new campaign is in full swing, Gordon, it's geared toward fixing Y2K problems. *Fear* sells. But with an uplifting spin. I'll be advertising in newspapers and on our website. The web designer is taking care of that too. I'll also have a new email campaign to send out to prospects. Vikram is helping me with the email distros; we've got a huge list. I'm also talking to a couple new experienced sales executives," Todd added.

Gordon nodded and forced a smile. "Okay, great." *How did Todd make this much progress on his own? I gave him sales and marketing just to occupy his ego and he's somehow flourishing.* "So, when are we going to meet them?"

"And how are we going to afford them?" Robert asked.

"I do have a little cash freed up if we need it," Gordon said. "But that's beside the point. Todd, what exactly is going on with the new salesmen?"

Todd flicked his tongue ring. "The beauty is that these aren't full time—mostly, they'll sell for commissions and points on the sale. To answer your question—yes, I will set up some meeting times. They'll fly into Omaha, and we can use Hank and Frank's office space for—"

"Fly? Why would we do that?" Robert asked.

"Don't worry about it. I'll take care of it guys, it's probably a formality. These old dudes are rock stars," Todd said.

"Okay. Can you please tell us more about who we're going to be looking at? I'm entitled to know, aren't I?" Gordon didn't like having to pry all this information, though he chalked up his feelings that Todd was withholding something to paranoia.

"Of course you are," Todd said. "C'mon, Gordon, you're acting like you think I'm trying to hide something. I'm telling you everything I know. Gabriel Chastain is based in San Francisco. He's done sales not just on the West Coast but also Europe. He has a background in product management and business development. Then I've got Eddie Calabrese coming in from New Jersey, covering the New York metro area. He's an experienced sales and account executive, not so much technology background but he's just a smooth operator."

Gordon nodded slowly. "Interesting cast of characters. We're going to be selling on both coasts?"

"I'll still cover Nebraska and the Midwest. Just leave the rest to me," Todd said.

He felt uneasy with the prospect, but he agreed. Todd was handling things better than he'd expected.

20/ BAY AREA I

Spring 1998

A friendship founded on business is better than a business founded on friendship
—John D. Rockefeller

Gordon arrived just in time for the JWorld opening remarks and keynote in the dauntingly large Moscone Center main hall. He managed to find a seat with Robert, Todd, and Vikram before the lights dimmed and the chatter softened to a mumble.

Strobe lights flashed.

"Are you ready for this!" blared the *Space Jam* theme.

Two fantastically unathletic men charged the stage, the tech giant CEO with a swinging ponytail followed by the balding middle-aged chief engineer. The chief engineer stumbled and nearly fell on his face. They botched a high five, missing hands and colliding forearms. If not for his thick glasses, the chief engineer would have taken a finger in the eye. After the CEO made his opening remarks, he presented a product roadmap. The crowd went mild.

The chief engineer returned to center stage, aimed the cannon like Bazooka Joe, and launched shrink-wrapped shirts into the crowd.

They're playing that stupid jam song again.

"Is that James Beck? It is! Dude, it is him. He designed one of the first Unix GUIs, introducing modern UI concepts that everyone ripped off," Robert exclaimed.

"Over here, James, this way!"

James Beck aimed the cannon toward them and fired a shot only two rows behind the Sagan team. Software developers dove, dogpiled, shoved. Soft bodies collided and conference chairs overturned and collapsed. It was no small effort for the priceless prize of a cheap imported T-shirt.

"Show's over, gents. Now let's go to the exhibit hall," Gordon said.

But he felt he lost his nerve at the sight of the expansive exhibition show with countless booths, ads, demos, exhibits, and showcases. *I'm not smart enough, not accomplished enough, to be here. Just take some of the free swag from the booths and don't make eye contact. Come on, I'm the CEO, right? I've made it to the big show.*

"Weren't we supposed to get a booth here, Todd?" Robert asked.

"Are you freaking kidding . . . You think we can afford a booth here? It's like a thousand dollars a booth-foot." Todd laughed.

"Do we have some business cards at least?"

"Oh yeah," Todd said. The Sagan team stopped and waited for him to pull out the stack from his backpack. "For you, and for you."

"These are nice!! *Robert Schroeder, CTO. Sagan Software.* Nice touch with the logo and slogan." Robert nodded approvingly.

"Yeah, I had our new graphic designer put these together for us. Don't you love them?"

"*Sagan Software. Solving the World,*" Gordon read from his card, "What the hell does that mean? That sounds absurd. I didn't approve this."

"Do I get some?" Vikram asked.

Todd handed him a stack. "Vikram, here's a few blank ones. You can write your name or whatever you want on them, homes."

"Todd, I don't remember approving these," Gordon repeated.

"This is what our graphic designer put together for us. You wanted them for the trip, Gordo," Todd said dismissively. "You weren't responding to those email proofs, so I made an executive decision."

"Yeah, you did," Robert said. "And it looks great!"

It wasn't a fight worth getting into, at least not here. A booth worker caught Gordon's eye and waved them over.

"Hey guys, how's it going today? Where are all of you from?" he asked.

"We're from Nebraska," Gordon said.

"I have a good friend from Omaha," the booth worker said. "What do you all do?"

But I'm a Lincolnite. Lincoln is a big little town and Omaha is a little big town.

Todd stepped forward. "We're a software development and consulting company."

"Oh, perfect. Perhaps you'd be interested in our project. We're working on one of the first Java IDEs. Do you program on Java?"

"Yes. And VB, JavaScript. We are polyglots," Vikram said.

"Yes, of course. Then you would be interested in an IDE, Integrated Development Environment. Yes? It helps you work on your project, edit code."

"Do you really need an IDE to write code? Isn't a text editor faster? Doesn't this additional software bog down the system?" Todd asked.

"I use VIM," Robert said.

A raucous disturbance stole their attention. A crowd of developers charged toward a booth near the end of their row.

"More free T-shirts!"

A mob of tech gurus and developers, the majority with six-figure incomes, fought mercilessly for free T-shirts. Gordon pressed into the dogpile of flabby engineers, until the sweatiness and body odor was unbearable. The T-shirts were running out quickly. Gordon could not endure.

They checked out a little more of the exhibition and then went to the cafeteria. The free soda bins in the lunch area were even more popular than free T-shirts. Developers double- or triple-fisted, stacking cans of caffeine.

"Did you guys get a chance to meet up with Chastain?" Robert asked as they sat down at an empty table.

"Yeah," Gordon said, trying to put on his best poker face.

Robert raised his eyebrows. "So I take it from that look on your face it didn't go well?"

"He seems like a douchebag to me." Gordon opened his free soda and took a sip. The meeting with Chastain, in Gordon's opinion anyway, had been something of a waste of time. They'd met up with him at some swanky restaurant with live jazz music and had spent the evening listening to Chastain try to smooth talk everyone as he bragged about his new boat and young girlfriends, all the while ordering cocktail after cocktail.

Vikram shrugged. "I liked him."

"Todd, is he a douchebag?" Robert asked.

"He's a bit of a douche, yeah. But, come on bro, what do you expect from a salesman?"

"I don't know, Todd. Maybe, at least, to be likeable?"

"How's this for likable," Gordon said. "At the end of all this wining, dining, and schmoozing, Chastain picks up the tab, he says, with his most French accent, 'No, no. Please, sir, I want to pay. My pleasure.' And then he puts down the corporate card we just gave him. I looked right at the card. The same Sagan Amex we gave him for prospecting."

"Okay, Gordon. Big deal. That's what it's for. M & E. Meals and entertainment," Todd said.

"Todd, did you miss my point? Why would he impress me? It is my company card. It's my freaking company paying for it."

"So, did you catch what he said about the prospect?" Todd said. "The proof is in the pudding. Rob, dog, I'm for real. He has a great lead here in San Fran. He's going to try to set up an in-person meeting while we're here."

"What he said is that he would *try*, but that it would be more likely a conference call. Seems like he's stalling to me," Gordon said. Again, he was overcome with the feeling that something was off but he couldn't articulate what it was.

21/ BAY AREA II
Spring 1998

There will be no more night.

—Revelation 22:5

"You got any Y2K?"

"Yeah, we want the rowdy shit."

It was incredible—they'd landed in San Francisco last Monday and people already knew about Y2K.

"How many you need? They're thirty each," Gordon said.

They had ventured to a nightclub after an evening of lavish San Francisco dot com company parties. Gordon looked down over the balcony from the third-story mezzanine. A DJ was spinning jazzy house music from the second level to the not-yet-crowded dance floor in the pit below. Robert and Gordon each held a new baby blue pill. Now that the Sagan business was behind them, they could get the real party started.

"You think Todd is acting strange?" Robert asked. "He seems detached. I know you weren't too happy with him making an executive decision with the business cards."

"He's Todd. I don't know. Would you ever want him hanging out with us? I think he left the first conference after-party with Vikram."

Another stranger approached them. "My friend in VIP wants to see you."

They followed him to a security guard, who let them through to a VIP table. Robert and Gordon sat and met the man who had requested their presence. A dressy young lady served skinny champagne glasses. Strobe lights flashed on the man's face, shining on his gold chains and peppered chinstrap beard. The hard tribal house vibrated the table.

"To what do we owe this honor?" Gordon asked nonchalantly.

"I want to know where you're getting your product. I hear it's the bomb," the VIP said.

"We're a software development company attending a tech conference," Robert said. "We offer software solutions, custom developed, not any specific product. But we could help you build your product."

"Relax—we know who you are. You know we know," the VIP said.

"All right, then, I'm listening," Gordon said.

"Cheers. Where do you get your fine product from? The rowdy shit. You know what I'm sayin'. You must not be local, or I'd know you. This is my club, my 'hood, you see. I don't have to play nice with all this olive branch shit. But I see that you're legit, clean-cut businessmen."

"My partner Robert is right. All our products are custom developed. We make it back home," Gordon said.

"I hear it's not even straight up E. That it's some crazy mix you got going on."

"Yeah, it's some wild trip all right. Cocktails."

"So, come on. You're at my nightclub, in my city. I'm being a good host. Tell me, what is it then? MDA and mescaline? The Bees?"

"Like I said, it's a secret family recipe. We can't share that. I shouldn't have said cocktails. It's not just a simple blend. That would be an insult. We've designed a new drug, like the Huey Lewis and the News song."

"I'd like to partner with you," the VIP said.

Gordon shook his head. "We're not looking for equal partners. But I could supply you with our product. Y2K."

"Should we be talking about this here?" Robert scratched his goatee and glanced over his shoulder.

"Gordon, tell your partner to relax. I trust everyone here at this table—on my word. And this music is too loud for anyone else to hear anything."

"So, you want me to open a new pipeline to the West?" Gordon asked.

"This is my town so I shouldn't have to ask. This is the easy way. You don't want to know the hard way."

"Where there's a pill there's a way. That's what we say with Y2K," Gordon said. He held out his arms like the statue in Rio.

They shook on it and arranged a contact. Gordon was over the moon. Finally, they were done with business.

"Shit man, we may close a deal in Cali before Chastain. What's up with that? Let's celebrate," Gordon said.

They each swallowed a baby blue Y2K pill. Gordon patted Robert on the shoulder and counted his lucky stars. *I am soaring to new heights. I'm making money on deals you won't believe. What started as back alley deals in jalopies transformed into California VIP room negotiations. That was like some gangster movie. If only Tonya could see me now. But she is a sheltered person and would not be proud of drug money. I would tell her all about Sagan Software and our brave new ventures. Coming from Silicon Prairie to meet people from 'The Valley', only for them to laugh while we assure them that Silicon Prairie is in fact a thing. And then making Silicon Prairie a real thing. Tonya would be so proud. I would tell her that.*

I would tell her what?

Gordon grasped the rail on the winding staircase. His vision blurred and his heart raced.

Just make it to the ground floor.

Overpowered by Y2K, he escaped reality to enter a brave new world, profoundly lost in the moment, lost in this world.

After soaring to new heights, he touched down on terra firma. A world of pounding beats and frenetic dancing. A mob of kindred spirits bonding to dance music. They formed a tight-knit group shoving aggressively to the center of the dance pit. Gordon exchanged fragmented sentences with a tall, athletic young man from Minnesota who thanked him profusely after borrowing a lighter. Gordon was obsessed with the man's clothes and his visor and the way he said his sweaty hair felt cool sticking out of the top. Gordon was unintelligibly effusive about the visor and decided to get one himself and said it would go well with his new haircut. The Minnesotan's jersey reflected mesmerizingly in the strobing lights. Gordon met many new friends and traded novelties somehow while still jumping around in the dance pit.

Robert finally came back into view and Gordon eagerly introduced him to the Minnesotan. He stared into the abyss past the edge of the crowd and panicked for water.

We must find water!

He grabbed someone on the dance floor and shouted, "We need water, comrade! Who's going to brave the storm for provisions?"

"What are you talking about? Are you crazy? What's wrong with you?"

What is wrong with me? Am I some degenerate? He's not part of our group. Robert shook him and pulled him back to the present.

"Let's go get a drink," he said, leading Gordon away from the crowd and toward the bar.

"Booze?" Gordon asked, horrified.

"No, orange juice."

They climbed up the winding staircase, better for their wear, gazed out at the dancing mob, and eventually sidled up to the bar. At first, Gordon sat on the barstool, clenching his teeth. He tasted his drink. *This is a screwdriver. With vodka. No, not what I want. Yeah, settle down. The other people at the bar seem to be minding their own business.*

A soft-cheeked young man who hardly appeared of legal drinking age took a seat next to Gordon. He was accompanied by a tall, thin young lady with creamy white skin—a stunning natural beauty. She became their center of gravity. Gordon looked closer at her childish face, soft lips, long limbs, and slender figure.

Robert was all over the place, searching for straws, napkins, and his composure. Gordon tried to spark a casual conversation with the couple without awkward staring. He lit a cigarette.

"You can't smoke here. It's the new law in California," the young man said.

"I'm sorry, man. Smoking law? I've never heard of such a thing." Gordon twitched around, searching for someplace to put out his cigarette. He hoped the bartender hadn't noticed.

"You guys aren't from here, are you?" the young man said. He looked more closely at Gordon, who had gone back to clenching his jaw. "You're high on something, aren't you?"

"Don't tell on us," Robert said.

"Oh, relax. We're cool. You guys seem harmless, anyway," the young man said.

"What's your name?" Robert asked the girl.

"I'm Betsie. And who are you?"

"I'm Gordon, and this is Robert. Where are you from?"

"Betsie is from Kansas and I'm from here. My name's Sebastian."

"No shit!" Gordon exclaimed. "We're from Nebraska. What are you doing here in California?"

"Can't you see," she said, laughing, "I'm with my boyfriend, Sebastian."

"She grew up in Kansas. But she's been modeling in New York for a couple years," Sebastian clarified. "We met in college at Pepperdine. When Betsie was young and clueless."

"Where is that?" Robert asked.

"Malibu."

"Wow, that sounds fancy," Gordon said.

"Yeah, Malibu is rad, but LA is a city with problems. Anyway, she just finished a shoot in New York. And, so, we're celebrating."

"We're celebrating too!"

"Apparently. It looks like it," Betsie said.

"Gordon, you look like you're tweaking hard. And Robert? You do too," Sebastian said.

"I've got the best rolls. These are designer drugs. Made in the USA. Made in Nebraska. You guys want to party with us?" Gordon asked exuberantly.

Sebastian put his arm around Betsie. "Sweetie, do you want to party tonight?"

Betsie pecked Sebastian on the cheek and blew Gordon and Robert a kiss.

"That means yes," Sebastian said.

He slid his drink across the bar and motioned for them to follow him outside. They walked a couple blocks to a paid parking lot. Gordon hooked them up with Y2K pills and Sebastian paid generously.

They followed him to a sharp-looking convertible, top down, and got in. Sebastian tore out, navigating deftly through the street blocks blasting the new Public Enemy song. Robert and Gordon elevated to a new level, beyond intoxication to full crystalized energy.

The convertible flew down the highway. Gordon sensed a rush of energy as the oncoming traffic whizzed by at arm's length. Giant vertical cables flashed and flickered as they started to cross the Golden Gate Bridge. They were flung further into the vortex. Vapor trails. A towering structure came toward them like a massive iron creature with short horns.

Gordon felt Sebastian downshift, drop the clutch, and punch the accelerator. The next bridge tower came toward them even faster. He winced as they shot between the legs. He looked up at the dizzying heights of the bridge tower.

We're going so fast I'm going to fly out of the car.

They accelerated into the vortex as they shot into a tunnel of darkness. Horns honked and reverberated, Betsie squealed with laughter, shouts bounced and echoed into a crescendo.

"Where the hell are we?" Robert asked.

"We're going to Sausalito. I have a little condo up there," Sebastian said.

"Salsa. Leto." Robert said. "Up?"

"Salsa," Gordon shouted. "Leto."

"Yeah, something like that," Betsie laughed.

"Holy shit, it is coming on now. This is some strong stuff," Sebastian said, breathing heavily.

The car slowed down to a crawl.

Betsie rubbed his shoulder. "Take your time honey."

The car snaked, swerved, and screeched up a hillside and pulled into a car port. Leading them into the condo, Sebastian turned on lights and music and flung keys onto the kitchen counter. They all shared a moment, gazing through the glass at the lights down the hill and across the bay on Belvedere Island. Sebastian showed them out to the patio to share a cigarette. Gordon was overwhelmed. Sebastian and Betsie were peaking on the first wave.

"This is amazing," Gordon said. "Thank you for this moment."

"No, Gordon, Robert. My new best friends. Thank *you!*"

How could it get any better than this.

I'm truly on top of the world now.

Robert was obsessed with Betsie, not sexually like an infatuation or crush, but as a goddess. A work of art. He marveled at her hands and smooth shiny hair. She tucked her hair behind her left ear, and it stuck out just a bit. He had never seen a perfect ear like that before then. The sum of the parts—from the curves of the helix and pits and the canyons and the soft dangling lobe—sculpted beauty. In short, Robert was having a good trip.

"So, what's it like to live in New York City? Must be expensive," Gordon said.

"Well, she doesn't have to pay for anything," Sebastian said.

"Be quiet, Sebastian. There are way too many people. And the traffic is bad. My apartment is so loud at night too. But I do love the social scenes. And the food. I just miss the outdoors. And I miss my family and my hometown. It is so quiet and peaceful there. And we had animals. I grew up with horses and a pond. I loved it."

"So, you miss Kansas then?" Gordon asked skeptically.

"Yes, of course I do."

"The tale of a country girl from Kansas turned New York City model. I'll never forget you, Betsie," Robert said.

Betsie smiled. "Aw, that's so sweet."

When they went back inside, Sebastian showed Gordon a large monitor screen mounted on the wall for playing music. A Winamp EQ glowed in auburn and tangerine while the track listing pulsed. Then graphics took over and geometric patterns shook and jived to the music.

"Who set this up for you?" Gordon asked.

"I had a friend do it for me for some artwork. It's a beta version of Winamp 2. That there is the new screensaver prototype."

"You're an artist then?"

"Oh no." Sebastian grinned and shook his head. "I'm an art dealer. I've been slowly working my way up in the art world, step by step. I'm from a family of art dealers."

I've never met an art dealer, not in Nebraska.

"What's that like?"

"I've always had a passion for art. It's all I know. My great uncle was an artist, and he did very well. But I don't have the gift. As a dealer, I survive. I follow my tastes and instincts," Sebastian said.

As a dealer myself, I have survived by following my own tastes and instincts.

"You like trance?" Sebastian asked, changing the song.

"We're house and techno junkies. Trance can be too poppy, you know, and trance anthems, drum rolls, are a bit cliché," Gordon said.

"Give this Oakenfold live mix a chance," Sebastian said.

Trance melodies peaked and dropped. Screen shapes pulsed and morphed. Bass thumped. Four on the floor. They danced as one. Nighttime lights smeared and rippled across the glassy cove. BT's "Flaming June" track charged and quaked from the speakers. A tsunami rushed in. The crashing wave of Y2K washed over them. Then a powerful tide pulled them out to deep sea. And then the sun rose and glimmered on the bay.

22/ EQUITY

Spring 1998

Capitalism is the legitimate racket of the ruling class.

—Al Capone

Gary seemed pleased with the latest demo. The Sagan team showed him advanced financial analysis features on the web app using Java Applets and other esoteric details beyond his technical know-how. They hoped that this meant he'd be agreeable to the offer they were about to make him.

"In terms of the buyout offer," Todd started, "you would remain a minority owner of the new company. So, you won't have a controlling interest."

"Yes, agreed," Gary said. "A residual stock owner. Minority share. That's what makes the most sense now. Let me know when you put this into writing."

"Would you be willing to share your marketing strategy with us today?" Gordon asked.

"If you're willing to share your independent analysis. Quid pro quo."

"Of course," Todd said. He glanced from Gary to Gordon. "This is not us versus you—we're on the same team now. This is a conversation between co-owners. Let's win together."

Todd handed out copies of their report. The analysis consisted of various graphs and figures such as license and revenue projections and other finance and marketing analysis used in the business case.

Gary looked it over. "I don't need to see any phony projections. We're all in agreement that we're going after the small fish, right?"

"We're going to segment the market, separate out the bigger firms, and target the day traders or smaller firms," Gordon said. "And that customer base will grow dramatically with the rise of the internet. You're going to see a lot more day traders by 1999."

Todd turned a page on the report. "Yes. As the research summary states here in section 3, electronic trading is a major growth area. E-trade went public in 1996. In St Louis, Scottrade forecasts tremendous growth potential in online trading. My Omaha contacts at TD Ameritrade are telling me to push all my chips out on the table."

"Well. Okay, boys. Then let me explain my side." Gary leaned back in the dining room chair, interlacing his fingers behind his head. "So, how do these amateur day traders compete against the professionals? All the big shot hedge fund managers, investment bankers, Wall Street traders, et cetera, subscribe to the Bloomberg Terminal. We're not going to beat out Bloomberg, but we can give them an affordable option. And I'm not just providing yesterday's closing price and public SEC filing info. Real time data, analysis with proprietary formulas, meaningful research, screeners, and much more." Gary released his hands and leaned forward, thumping his fist on the dining room table. "And we're not talking about investment bankers doing one hundred million dollar trades. Bloomberg costs, what, like at least twenty-thousand a year? Let me tell you, it is NOT user-friendly or intuitive. Heck, it has its own special keyboard. Vikram said the other day that it requires a special installation and server set up. My software—our software—will work like a web application, right Robert? You boys were brilliant with that idea. This is something else."

"Todd's going to arrange a meetup with Hank and Frank," Gordon said.

"Hank and Frank?" Gary smirked. "They sound like a can of pork and beans. Who are they?"

"Remember? Henry Sherman and his lawyer and partner Frank," Todd said.

"Oh, right. King Henry of Omaha, of course."

Gary stood from the table, wadded up the market report, and posted up, shouting, "Pump fake, jump shot from the perimeter. Swoosh! Three!"

"So, Gary, what is your exit strategy?" Todd asked.

"You're asking me that now?! While I'm discussing the process of selling out? I hope that we all get to sell out again. And at a much higher price, through acquisition."

"Why not hold out longer, Gary? Why are you willing to trade us majority ownership then? I mean, we're grateful the opportunity but—"

"I usually pour myself one hundred percent into something for about two or three years. Day in, day out, twenty-plus hours a day. I'm a perfectionist. Then I move on to something else. I'm happy to be a silent owner. And then I can move on to my next pursuit," Gary said.

"Well, Hank Sherman is the right person to take this forward," Todd said.

"Anyway, enough of that. Now the year 2000 bug is going to be cataclysmic, I hope you boys aren't leaving all your money in the banks. Just think. It would just take one erroneous nuclear missile launch and then we're talking World War Three," Gary ranted.

Gordon reflected on his own illicit side hustle of Y2K pills and prayed that would also not lead to calamity.

"Stay a while, at least until my wife comes home. So, Monika Lewinsky, huh? That Bill Clinton—"

They cut off Gary's Midwestern goodbye.

"Have a nice day, Gary."

{-----}

Gordon was elated by Sagan's progress and wanted to celebrate his achievements. He felt so good about things, he decided to give Tonya a call. Their prior "date" couldn't even be counted as such, with Ashley tagging along. He wanted to give it one last chance before he gave up.

Tonya seemed pleased to hear from him when she picked up the phone, and Gordon told her business was going well and he'd like to take her out. She asked if they could go shopping.

"It'll just be the two of us," she added. "I'm sorry that the date got messed up because of my poor planning."

"Hey, that's all right," Gordon said. "It was nice to meet your friend; I hope she had a good time."

Tonya laughed. "Oh, she did . . ."

Gordon had been through hospitalized illness, beatings by bullies, and pulled many all-nighters at work—but nothing prepared him for a full day of shopping with Tonya. Shoes, dresses, coats, jewelry, blouses, sandals, purses, handbags. Trying on everything. Asking Gordon, under duress, what he thought. Gordon was dehydrated and felt like he was running a fever. *How many purses or handbags does someone need? Do they have to match each outfit? Why not find a bag that matches everything?*

"So, you like country music?" Gordon asked as they walked out of yet another shoe store.

"Yeah," Tonya said.

"What kind of country music?"

"I don't know. Whatever they play on the radio."

"Would you ever want to go to a club and see my friend Michael spin some records? He's a DJ. Mostly house but some techno music."

She made a face. "Oh, I don't like techno. That I do *not* like."

"That's fine. But anyway. You went to a dance club with Ashley. Did they play dance music?"

"Yeah, but I'm not there for the music. I go there to hang out with my friends and meet people."

Gordon sighed. Clearly, there was a disconnect. He followed her into another store and gazed across the endless clothes hanging on display, at the circular clothing racks he used to hide inside as a child. He wished he could crawl back in now.

After they left the store with yet another shopping bag, Tonya said she was hungry, so they headed over to the food court.

"So, like, what does your company do?"

"Software development. We build custom applications and do web hosting and IT. Computer stuff."

"Yeah, that sounds hard. And boring too."

"It's more exciting than it sounds. We're on the verge of really making it. Do you know where you want to be and where you want to go when you grow up?" Gordon asked. They sat at a small table underneath an indoor tree. Tonya took a long sip of her soda.

"After I meet the right guy, and then get married, I want to have a family and raise children," she said. "What about you? I mean, you're already grown up, with your own company and everything."

Gordon smiled. "Honestly? I hope my work takes me away from Nebraska. I can't decide whether to go to New York or California. Either would be better. Anywhere but here."

"What's wrong with Lincoln anyway?" Tonya asked, raising an eyebrow. "I love it here."

She said it with no sense of irony, though Gordon wondered if perhaps she was just messing with him. "What's in Lincoln?"

"My family is here. It's a nice town. It's clean and safe. My friends are here too. What's in New York or California?"

"Everything. Anything you can imagine. Have you even been to New York City?"

"I've been there once. I didn't like it."

"What? You didn't like New York City?!" Anyone who liked shopping as much as she did would have to love NYC, as far as he was concerned.

"New York is so dirty and so crowded. Ew. The buildings were covered in graffiti. Everything seemed sketchy or downright dangerous. No thanks."

"What? You must be crazy."

"Excuse me, mister computer company big shot. You don't have to talk down to me."

"Do you want another pop refill? Or a pretzel?"

"No, I'm all set."

"Would you still like to have dinner tonight?"

Tonya yawned and leaned back in her chair. "No, I'm too tired."

It was a quiet ride home. Gordon was exhausted from pushing that rock up a hill. He gradually admitted to himself that the reality of Tonya was not matching his dreams.

"I asked for a tour of the operation, Damian. Why's that so complicated?" Gordon bounced around in the back seat as the Ford Galaxie motored down the country road.

"Don't look at me," Dino said, "I'm not involved in the supply side. Damian runs the operation. I'm just a distributor. Shit, I'm going to have to wash my car again." They tore up more dust as he accelerated.

"Show me the lab, Damian," Gordon said again, slapping his hand on the back of Damian's seat.

"I'm not gonna show you," he said. "It's way out there in Otoe County. Don't take it personally—I'm protecting you, protecting us. You need to be able to pass a lie detector test. If you don't know you can't tell anyone."

Gordon sat back in his seat. *Why the hell won't he just take me there. Something is not right.*

Dino stroked his braided goatee.

"I don't know how else to explain it," Damian said.

"Well, where are we going then?" Gordon asked.

"We're going to an old farmhouse, man. This location will be like a buffer. There's an ample supply of merchandise in a shed right on the farm property. You can go get more stuff any time, man, you know what I'm sayin'. You just need to let me know what you take. Dino made an extra key for you," Damian said.

"Do you drive this big hooptie out here all the time? That'll bring some unwanted attention," Gordon pointed out.

"We have an old pickup with a bed cover and a toolbox. I usually take that out to the lab," Damian said.

"Do you cover your identity as well? Is the old truck tagged with an untraceable plate?"

"Uh, yeah, sure, it is," Damian said.

"Damian, be careful that you are not identified. Get a plate that can't be traced. Dino, that's your department."

The old farmhouse sagged like it had never recovered from the Great Depression. The house and its surroundings were obscured by giant old growth trees. An old windmill inched creakily.

A shed—packed with antiques, old tools, dilapidated furniture, farm equipment, magazine piles, dust, and cobwebs—hid a vintage freezer. Dino cleared their way through clutter and opened the old freezer, revealing a pile of black gym bags. Gordon lifted a bag out of the heap. He pulled the zipper and, with sweaty hands, grabbed a few pill bottles.

They walked briskly back to the Ford Galaxie. Pills rattled in Gordon's cargo pants.

"Good work, Dino. This will do," Gordon said.

"Thanks, boss," Dino said.

23/ LITTLE DEBBIE

Summer 1998

We're concerned about the potential disruption of power grids, telecommunications, and banking services.

—Sherry Burns, CIA

Senior Special Agent Parker looked at his reflection in the driver side mirror of the unmarked car. At thirty-seven, Parker was in great shape, with a square jaw and athletic shoulders. His receding hairline was all that showed his age. His junior partner Special Agent Rasmussen, sat in the passenger seat.

"Let's assume that Damian Charlock is the kingpin," Rasmussen said. "That *he* is the main manufacturer that's supplying the product, or he's directly in contact with the main supplier. You think that narrative holds water?"

"No, I don't think so, Raz. But he'll bring us to Brendan, who will bring us to the supplier." Parker was sure of it.

"What's Damian's story anyway?"

"Male, twenty-two. He is a, well, *was*, a chemistry major. He has the training and skills to be dangerous. You've heard everything that I have on him." The two men got out of the car and walked the short distance to a nearby picnic table and opened their lunch sacks.

"What about Robert? He's the brightest of the bunch," Rasmussen said, extracting a foil-wrapped sandwich.

"Straight-A student, valedictorian. Nothing on Robert. He's clean. Probably just part of the legitimate business, like Todd Wallace. And Todd's father, Dennis Wallace, is a pillar of the community." Parker unwrapped the plastic wrap on his own sandwich and took a bite.

"I brought the tape player. We could play it here while we eat," Rasmussen suggested.

Parker and Rasmussen munched away on their sandwiches like cattle chewing their cud. Rasmussen opened a bag of snack cakes.

"You shouldn't eat so many of those processed desserts. Too much sugar and saturated fat. Besides you're making a mess and attracting more flies," Parker complained.

"God, I mean, gosh, I can't help it. I really like these coffee cakes and donut sticks. Who do you think does it better, Hostess or Little Debbie?"

Parker gave Rasmussen a withering look.

"Only two grams of saturated fat in the coffee cakes. That's nothing. The donut sticks have eight grams," Rasmussen said.

"But how many grams of sugar? Why don't you just give me a donut stick if I'm going to have to sit here and watch you eat them and go on about them."

"Nineteen grams."

"Anyway, you can play the tape already. Just stop it if someone approaches."

Rasmussen pressed play on the handheld cassette player. A television in the background, voices mumbling, a microwave beeping, a door closing. They listened to an asinine conversation between Damian and a friend about what they were going to watch on TV.

Rasmussen fast forwarded, played, fast forwarded. Repeat.

"Do they ever go outside and do anything or just sit and watch TV?" Rasmussen asked.

"Well, what do you expect, Raz, that's the tape from the living room. Why don't you change the tape?"

Rasmussen switched out a tape and pressed play.

"Should I dye my hair again?"

"I don't care. I like you colorful. What do you want, mayo or mustard?"

"Like, maybe purple or violet. I can see my roots already."

"Welcome to Sonic. Can I take your order?"

Fast forward, play, fast forward. Repeat.

"Are you going back to the trailer again to see Brendan tomorrow? I've got some more friends who want to sample your latest concoction."

"Wait, pause the tape. What is that girl talking about—concoctions?" Rasmussen asked.

"Must be Debbie," Parker said. "Damian's lover. Deborah Bailey. Her mother is Crystal Bailey, age thirty-six. No father in the picture. Must have been a teenage mother. Apparently, she knows more than we suspected. I'm calling it. She's their weakest link."

"Leaves don't fall far from the tree. Well, let's get the little bitch. Why not? She'll take us to Brendan. She's got no cover." Rasmussen stood up from the picnic table, flinging crumbs in the air.

"You don't know her, Special Agent. Never de-humanize anyone. We're the good guys. Never forget that. Let's go talk to Debbie."

They threw their trash out and walked back to the car.

"*Little* Debbie." Rasmussen laughed.

Parker gave Rasmussen a piercing senior agent glance.

{-----}

Debbie approached the little wooden homemade front porch to her mother's trailer, where her mom was standing with an ex-boyfriend, leaning on the 2x4 railing, sipping a can of Busch Light.

"I don't know why they haven't moved that goddamn dumpster yet," her mother said, pointing toward the neighboring trailer.

"How much garbage ya think they could've packed in that little trailer? To need to fill this here full-sized dumpster. Jeez. Anyhow, hello, Debbie. I was just about to head on out," her mother's ex-boyfriend said. Debbie couldn't remember his name.

"They'd cleaned up and moved out months back so the trailer should be empty by now. Look what the cat dragged in!" Debbie's mom said. "Where the hell have you been all day?"

"It's Friday," Debbie said. "I've been at school all day. Where else?"

"Who's that weird boy who dropped you off? Why's he dressing like a black fella? You're not still going with him, are you?"

Debbie rolled her eyes. "Yes, Mom. I'm still 'going with him.' Damian is my *boyfriend*. He's a hell of a lot smarter than the guys you bring home. He's going to graduate from college soon."

"He acts like a druggie freak if you ask me."

"I didn't ask you. At least he has plans. And he says he will make his plans with me by his side."

Her mother snorted. "I had plans. But guess who spoiled them plans?"

"Don't you dare—"

"I know men, too. I know a hell of a lot more about them than you. You're a dreamer like your father. Always a dreamer never a doer. I don't want you to end up with a deadbeat like him. Older men go after younger women for one thing, you know. Just one thing. I had a cute ass too when I was young, and don't you forget it." Her mother brought the beer can up to her mouth, tipped it back.

"Excuse me," Debbie said, slipping past them.

The ex-boyfriend left and her mother followed her inside. The trailer park culture was nothing like Todd Wallace's neighborhood, or even Damian's. Unlike the big houses with groomed yards and privacy fences, the trailer park dwellers would talk, gossip, grill, drink, party, fight, and sleep together. It was not unusual for Debbie to enter a neighbor's trailer unannounced, walk past parents and grandparents in the living room, and pop into a girlfriend's bedroom. The teenage boys roamed in droves.

Someone knocked firmly three times on their door.

"You gonna get up off your ass and answer that?" Debbie's mother asked.

"You gonna start the mac and cheese yet?" Debbie said. She pushed up off the couch and opened the door, startled by the sight of two casually dressed strangers.

"Hello, my name is Senior Special Agent Parker, and this is Special Agent Rasmussen," one of the men said. They revealed their credentials. "Can we come in?"

Debbie glanced around the neighboring trailers to see if anyone saw them. She was relieved to see the car they drove was unmarked. She let them in, turned off the TV, and seated them on the couch. Rasmussen had to make space to set his clipboard on the coffee table.

"Oh, Jesus Christ, Debbie, now what'd you get yourself into?" her mother exclaimed.

"If Deborah is willing to cooperate, it will help her chances in staying out of trouble. Debbie, would you like to take a ride with us to our Lincoln Resident Office where we can talk through all this?" Parker asked.

"Deb, whatever kinda trouble you got yourself into, you shouldn't have to go down for it. I ain't got no future. Don't worry about me. But I've been hoping for a future for you. So, don't spoil it all for that boy," her mother said.

"Your mother is offering sound advice, Deborah," Rasmussen said.

Parker glanced toward the kitchen, at the mac and cheese box, pot of water, and wet bag of hot dogs. "We're sorry to spoil your dinner," he said. "Special Agent Rasmussen will offer you a bite to eat on the car trip."

Debbie peered out the backseat window all the way to the office. She saw Damian's truck parked at a convenience store and realized how close of a call it was for her. And now it seemed that danger was closing in on Damian, too.

24/ NOT SO GREAT EXPECTATIONS

Summer 1998

Heaven knows we need never be ashamed of our tears.
—Charles Dickens

Gordon made his way, with Tonya and her friends, to one crowded college bar after another, like wild animals. He had a hard time keeping track of Tonya and her friends pushing through the mob. As soon as Gordon found them near the backyard bar, Tonya or one of her girlfriends would request that he go procure them another round of drinks.

He sat on the sticky bar stool and forced down another mixed drink of gut rot. He thought it might take the edge off, or at the very least dull the realization that he was nothing more than a glorified waiter for these girls. The more fun they had, the more out of place he felt.

What am I doing here? The question flashed on repeat as people socialized all around him. Whenever he tried to engage Tonya in conversation, he'd get a brief, sometimes one-word only response before she turned away and continued her conversation, laughing and joking with her friends. He even tried asking Tonya if she would marry him if they were single and old and she said, nonchalantly, "Sure." Eventually, he volunteered to drive them home, but not before buying them fast food.

Was he being persistent or just pathetic? He was at a loss for what more he could do for Tonya. When it came to dating, apparently, he was not going to fare much better than he had with his college courses.

{-----}

"We already know it's Damian. We know he has a lab. We know he's cooked up all of this. Deborah, we need you to do the right thing. Tell us where it is," Senior Special Agent Parker said.

"I don't know anything about any lab. I already told you. I swear," Debbie pleaded.

"We know about Y2K. Don't you think I can tell when you're lying?"

"I said I don't know anything about no lab."

"Then just tell us something then. Where does Damian go to work? Where does he go when he's alone? Any place that he frequents. Any general direction or lead that could guide us to the lab."

"How would I know where he goes when he's alone? I don't keep tabs on him. Listen, you guys already know so much stuff. I'm telling you—if there was a lab, I would probably know about it. But I don't."

"Don't play dumb with us," Parker said. "We're talking about MDMA, methamphetamines. The hard stuff. And we know they're developing new drugs."

"I swear on my grandmama's grave. If there was like a lab, like a building, or a trailer, or something where he's makin' stuff, then, I would know about it," Debbie said.

"A trailer. Okay, right," Rasmussen said, writing something down on a clipboard.

"Where's he getting the drugs then? We have you on tape, Debbie," Parker said, nudging the tape recorder on the table.

"All I know is that Damian and Dino work together on all kinds of shit. Maybe he got it from him."

"Dino is his street name. What is Dino's real name, Deborah?" Parker asked.

"I'm pretty sure it's Brandon or Brendan. They all grew up together. Damian, Brendan, and them," Debbie said.

"Brendan and them. Right," Rasmussen said, penning another note.

"Wait. Are you recording all this talking too?" Debbie asked.

"Yes. We always record our interviews. Standard procedure."

"Am I in trouble?"

"Not necessarily. Not if you keep cooperating."

"Now do you want to be a witness or a defendant?" Rasmussen asked.

"Defendant? Hold on, I want to know my rights. I'd like to talk to my lawyer."

"Okay, Deborah," Rasmussen said.

Parker paused the tape. They left the room.

"She lawyered up. That wasn't the smartest question, Raz," Parker said.

"She must be protecting herself from something then."

"She doesn't know anything about the lab."

"Maybe there is no lab."

Parker took a deep breath. "You think there is an ecstasy fairy leaving pills under their pillows?"

"No, sir."

"But unfortunately, I believe her. She knows all about the drug enterprise and she's used with Damian. But she doesn't know about the lab," Parker said. "We'll let her go—for now. We know where to find her, she can't go too far."

{-----}

Debbie stepped out of the unmarked building and dizzily walked down the concrete steps. She bolted for the bushes, leaned over, and spit up. She held back, spit, drooled, inhaled shakily, and then vomited profusely. Her eyes watered. She walked a few more blocks, sat on the curb, rested her head on her arms, and tried to gather her wits. She'd go to Jennifer's.

Debbie climbed up the doorsteps and throttled the door.

"Come in, Debbie. You don't look well," Jennifer said when she answered the door.

"Thanks for meeting with me. I didn't know who to talk to. I don't have anyone." Debbie began to cry.

"Oh, sit down. What's wrong?"

Debbie took a shaky breath and then recounted the interrogation with the special agents. "I love Damian, but I know he's in trouble. I just don't know what to do."

"Can you ask your parents for help?"

"It's just my mom and me. My mom will just say, 'I told you so'."

Jennifer gave her a sympathetic look. "You poor thing. I'll get you more tissues."

"My mom will tell me I never listened to her. I feel so stupid," Debbie sobbed.

"You're not stupid. It wasn't anything you did," Jennifer said.

"And I don't want to get you and Robert involved."

"Robert has stayed true and distanced himself from all of this. I trust that he's made good decisions. And it has nothing to do with me. Debbie, I think you need a lawyer."

"I don't have any money. I told those guys that I'm talking to my lawyer. But I don't have a lawyer and I'm broke. Just look at me." Debbie wiped at her eyes with the back of her hand. "And on top of everything else—I'm late."

Jennifer's eyes widened. "Well . . . you need to relax and calm down. You don't need any more stress. Don't people who can't afford a lawyer get assigned a public defender? You'll be okay. We'll be here for you."

"Really, I don't want to spoil things for everyone."

"You poor thing. Come here."

Another wave of nausea washed over Debbie. She brought her hand up to her mouth. "Is there a bathroom, I think I'm going to throw up again."

She followed Jennifer down the hallway and made it just in time.

25/ THE WEIGHT OF WATER

Fall 1998

We do in all honesty hate this world.

—Marshall Applewhite, *Heaven's Gate*

Daybreak crept through the dusty blinds into the bedroom. Gordon was coming down from a long night. He noticed three other stragglers, two sitting on blankets, and one partially lying in a sleeping bag, having a muted conversation. Gordon struggled to sit up from where he'd been sprawled on the floor. He felt awful.

"I wish I could just crawl under a rock," one guy said, covering his head with a blanket.

"I've been depressed all winter, and it hasn't gotten any better," another said. He looked at the girl seated next to him. "How is your son doing?"

"He's doing good. He's growing up so quickly. He's so big now," she said.

Gordon watched as she pulled a wallet-sized portrait from her purse and passed it around, tarnished from too many hard nights.

"He's been living with my parents while I'm between jobs. So, I get to visit him when I want to. But, you know, I haven't been getting along with my parents at all. It's like they don't want anything to do with me," she said plaintively.

"Well, I don't want anything to do with my parents either. I was their biggest mistake."

"Are you the black sheep too?"

"What's the point?"

"Of what?"

"Of any of this."

Gordon let the conversation drift over him until he heard his name. "What's that?" he said blearily.

"I was just asking how you were feeling," one of the guys said.

"Fine," Gordon said hoarsely.

"Those Y2Ks were bad ass rolls. You gonna hook us up tomorrow night too?"

"You mean tonight?" the girl said. "You were having fun last night, Gordon. You were bouncing off the walls."

He smiled weakly. "Yeah, good times." He could barely remember what happened. Loud music, a cramped dance floor in front of a sofa and coffee table. Mostly darkness. Neon lights with tracers. And drinking water out of the sink. Yes, he remembered holding water glasses under the kitchen faucet. Other people filled up glasses, too. And as they filled them to the brim, they could not feel the weight of water. They were amazed by this.

Gordon had made all kinds of new friends from his dealings but he never knew if they were truly friends or just using him as a drug hookup. In his gut, he felt he had made a mistake giving away pills to the apartment people rather than selling them at market price. Yet, as with the previous night, it made him a welcome guest.

Which Gordon needed, because Robert had been pulling away, distancing himself from the scene. He would never tell Gordon what to do, but he had warned him to be careful and not go too far to the dark side. He hoped Todd and his other business associates would never see him in this state. His mouth was parched, his whole body ached. If there was a dark side, this was surely it.

{-----}

In the early evening, Gordon returned to that same bleak apartment building where they had partied all night. He walked the creaky wooden steps to the right apartment and glanced through a window. *Nobody is home. Don't knock, not just yet.* He walked down the stairs and out to the back alley to have a cigarette. At the far end of the block, some boys kicked a soccer ball. A van pulled up and parked, but it was just a family unloading groceries. Gordon wondered if the family had overheard their music and partying. If the party had been a nuisance and disturbed them all night.

Gordon sat under the steps in the breezeway and rested his arms on his knees. He felt time slow down for a moment of dark introspection. He could not decide whether to knock on the door yet. *Everything is fine. They had invited me to return tonight. Be patient. Just wait for dusk to set. Or, if I see someone that I recognize return home then I can approach them. Maybe they are already in there and just resting.*

Gordon finally decided to walk up the stairs to the apartment. He knocked on the door cautiously. He knocked again. He heard rustling and footsteps inside leading to the front door. The door opened just a crack until the door chain caught. The apartment dweller peeked out with sleepy half-opened eyes.

"Hey, I was just napping," he croaked, "Who are you looking for?"

"I'm not sure," Gordon said, "I was invited back by, uh—"

"Uh, oh yeah. They're not here now. Sorry bro, but I'm trying to get some sleep. I have to work the doors at Jack's 'til close tonight," he said.

"Do you know when they're coming back?" Gordon asked.

"I've got no idea, bro," he said.

"Thanks." Gordon heard him pull the chain lock and turn the deadbolt.

{-----}

Gordon sat in his car, which had turned into his fortress of solitude. There was a lonely pit in his guts. He cruised past an unlit porch where Robert's old roommate Michael often DJ-ed house parties. He flipped to the next station.

"*In this day and age,*" the man on the radio was saying, "*we've got computers running everything for us. Computers are operating healthcare, transportation, power, water, agriculture, and manufacturing. Computers are even flying jet airplanes for us. I bet man is fixin' to take and make computers that drive you to church on Sunday morning. But computers ain't God's work. No, no. They* are man's work. This ain't God's intelligent design. This is man's imperfect, fallible design."

Laughter.

That's not funny at all.

The voice on the radio continued, "And when man designed these electronic thingamajigs. Ones and zeros spinning around and around. Tiny electrons moving so fast and fantastically. Well, these men didn't even make enough space for one or two of these here electrons to handle the year 2000. That wasn't God's infallible plan, y'all, that was man's flawed plan. Let me tell you about God's plan. 'Then I saw a new heaven and a new earth, for the first heaven and the first earth passed away, and there was no longer any sea.' Revelation, Chapter 21. Amen.

"America has been living a century of sin. Men are living together in sin. Our defenseless, unborn babies are being murdered every day. And this century of sin is closing in on itself. And all them so-called state-of-the-art computers are going to fail us. My brothers and sisters, we have got to prepare ourselves. We've got to prepare our souls. Amen. And our family homes. These are unprecedented times."

The radio show cut to a female host. "You were listening to the Reverend Jimmy Powell. For only $17.95 we will mail you Dr. Powell's 'Year 2000 Christian Home Preparation Guide' on VHS tape with a free brochure. Just call our toll-free number at 1-800—"

Gordon turned the radio off and thumbed through his CD wallet, keeping one eye on the road. Four CDs per page, covers on the back. He pulled out a good electronic mix to find a bit of solace. The dance track by Cevin Fisher. He said music saved my life, and without it, I would not know what I would do. And Gordon felt that same despair. It scraped him to the bone. The heavy beats gave flashbacks of the night before. Sinking, hollow gut feeling. Joy and pain. Guilt from taking more than a fair share of pleasure.

He eventually returned home and walked down the old cellar stairs into the dark basement. He reflected on the work that was going on with Sagan. Their trivial Y2K software projects starkly contrasted all the fear mongering. The struggling new opportunities and promising equity in Gary's venture. In his altered state, he felt dirty and paranoid thinking about legitimate work. Oh, to carry the weight of the Y2K drug operation, day in and day out. He pushed back the worries of his criminal enterprise to the darkest depths of his soul. It was no wonder that he self-medicated to ease the fear and pressure.

He suddenly remembered a personal stash of cocaine he had hidden for a rainy day. He dug in his closet, pulled out the empty puzzle box, and found the eight ball. He locked himself in his room, cut it, sniffed, cut it, sniffed.

Minutes racing, hours passing.

Pacing. Shadow boxing.

Turn music on, turn it off.

Look in the mirror. Wild-eyed.

You are nothing but dust and to dust you shall return.

Gordon licked the CD cover clean. He tasted the bitter chemical powder that quickly numbed his mouth. He fashioned a white pen tube to his nose to sniff any remaining morsels. He crawled around the floor and searched methodically through the carpet. Gordon even canvased the floor in the bathroom. He desperately sniffed specks up the pen tube to his nose. Anything remotely white.

That last one stung.

Just run some water through the pipes.

He grabbed several beer cans from the basement fridge and took them back to his room. He put on some headphones and listened to classic rock. He chugged a beer and licked the front of his teeth.

Have I achieved my dreams?

Is this making it big time?

His thoughts spun. His heart raced. And then there was no more night.

{-----}

When Gordon woke the next day, it was early afternoon. Beer cans littered the coffee table. Damian was on the couch, watching TV. Apparently, he had unsheathed one of the novelty Japanese swords they had purchased in San Francisco's Chinatown. He barely remembered, deep in paranoia, trying to prop the sword up to guard the stairway.

For display only. Thank God they're not sharpened.

He felt drained and all ate up inside. He recoiled as Damian lit a joint and offered him a hit. Gordon tried to hide his irritation as he declined the offer.

"I didn't mean to sleep so late," he said. Damian showed no signs of moving. "I'm going to head out for a little bit."

He drove over to Robert's new place and was greeted at the door by a feisty hound dog. *Am I at the right house?*

"Come on in," Jennifer said. The dog jumped up on Gordon, trying to lick him.

"Thanks for giving us all Monday mornings off," Robert said. "We still need to get that meeting set up with Gary. Oh, that's Betsie. We adopted her from the shelter a week ago."

Gordon rubbed Betsie's soft floppy ears. He got down onto the floor with the dog, who kept trying to give him kisses. She flopped down and rolled over, asking for a belly rub, which he obliged. She wagged her tail happily.

If I could just keep a hold on this little doggy, I might feel better today.

"Have a long night?" Jennifer asked.

"Oh," Gordon said. "You know. I thought I'd stop by and see if maybe you guys wanted to hang out or something."

Gordon tried to make himself at home by rubbing Betsie's tummy.

"Well, Gordon," Jennifer said, glancing at Robert. We were just about to go to the dog park. It's a beautiful day outside."

"Do you want to come with us?" Robert asked cautiously.

As much as he was enjoying Betsie's company now, the idea of going to a dog park was more than Gordon felt he could handle right now. He walked out with them, watched them all get into the car and drive off.

So, it's Robert, Jennifer, and Betsie now. That sounds lame. Why would he want to sit around and watch television and play with a dog? That's like something old people would do. Robert is still in his early twenties, and he already wants to turn into an old boring couple.

Yet Gordon knew this was his jealousy talking. He'd have to settle for driving around and listening to music, alone.

{Part 3}

26/ BLUE MONDAY
Winter 1998–1999

The question is not will there be disruptions, but how severe the disruptions will be.

—Senate Special Report on Y2K, February 1999

We need to save seven. They're going to fall in. No, you don't understand. Gordon rolled over and covered his head with a cool pillow.

Save seven what?

Just a dream.

The bedroom was darkness but for a sliver of gray seeping underneath his door. He remembered sleepwalking a couple times before falling asleep again. He had no idea what time it was. His computer mp3 player cycled through the nighttime playlist. The singing, chirping, and scuttling of a rainforest teeming with insects, birds, and monkeys. The drumming rainstorm calming into whispering drip-drop. This was his place of solace.

Gordon's throat and nose were sore. His head pounded. He felt a pressure pushing up on his upper throat, like he had been hooked and his entire body weight tugged from the roof of his mouth. His head was drained, as much from exhaustion as pain. He felt a sense of paralysis throughout himself.

A sinking feeling reminded him that it was Monday again and he had things to do. But he had given the company the day off on Mondays. He tossed and turned. He shut the world out for a while longer. He threw the blankets off and—in a fit of anger and cursing—flung himself out of bed.

He went back to Robert's, hoping for a better reception this time than when he'd been there last week. He found his friend sprawled on the couch in his boxers and t-shirt, catching an episode of *Law & Order*. Gordon was relieved that Jennifer was not there.

"Yo, dude. What's up?" Robert asked.

"I need your help with something today," Gordon said.

"Man, Gordo. We're worried about you. You've been pretty hard on yourself."

"Worried about what?" Gordon said.

"You need to be more careful. That stuff is hard on you. And, you know, it can affect others too." Robert eyed him. "You were looking pretty rough the last time you were here. You're not looking much better today."

Gordon's head felt foggy. "Damn Rob, is this an intervention?"

"Relax, Gordon. We love you, man. I'm just trying to help." Robert patted Gordon on the back. Gordon hunched over and covered his face.

Hide your pain. Push it down in a deep dark hole.

"I'm on the edge, Rob. But, c'mon, we've all been doing drugs. You too, right?"

"Yes, but you know better. You are *better* than this. Don't get high by yourself. And don't get high on your own supply."

"I know. There's a certain decorum with E and rave drugs. There's a respect for their power and balance with the world. Balance your mind, body, and soul." Gordon only wished it was that easy.

"We're techies not druggies," Robert said. "We had some fun times, sure, but we need to be more careful now. We have so much more to lose. Sagan Software is on the rise. Your company, Gordon, our company, is a real success!"

Gordon knew he was in a precarious position. But Robert was right.

"We do have something to lose now. So, I need your help."

"Anything," Robert said immediately.

"So, Gary believes the year 2000 problem is real. He's preparing for doomsday. He's building an underground saferoom, isn't he?" Gordon asked.

"Umm, yeah, like a bunker," Robert said.

Gordon took a deep breath and exhaled. "Then I need to prepare too. I need to bury a box of my primo Y2K pills here."

"What?! It's not even—Why do you need to do that?"

"Remember, Gary told us to bury cash, or even better, gold, and other supplies. Y2K will be better than cash. Better than gold," Gordon said.

Robert looked at him incredulously. "You're listening to Gary? Gordon, you've officially lost it." They stared at each other for several long moments. So long that Gordon thought Robert was going to refuse. "Fine," Robert said. "Fine. Now you'll owe me. Next time, *you* will be helping *me*. I won't forget it."

They found a spade and a shovel in the garage and went to the back-yard.

This will seem too suspicious. We can't just dig a hole in the middle of yard and bury something.

"We can't just start digging out there for no reason," Gordon said. "First, let's make a cover story. How about we're a couple guys gardening." They stared into the thicket of bushes and trees. "Even if it is the middle of winter."

"It's been a mild one, at least. The ground won't be frozen." Robert gazed around the yard. "I'd like to make a little path here," he said, pointing. "So, you could go from the lawn into the bushes."

"And we could get some stone steps," Gordon added.

"A little path."

"And then bury a box underneath one."

"Exactly. I have just the right box in my garage. We can get the stepping stones at the hardware store."

They got right to work after they returned from the store. It felt good to engage in physical labor. After they placed the first of the stepping stones into the ground, they took a break and admired their handywork.

"Hello there, gentlemen," a voice said. It was Robert's octogenarian neighbor, peering through the chain link fence. Her hunched figure trembled when she spoke. She wore a bathrobe and still had curlers in her hair.

"Hello, Mrs. Van Kirk. How are you today?" Robert asked.

"Above ground," she said.

Gordon felt a bittersweet pang. She was enjoying the day while he— young, successful, healthy—hadn't even been sure he'd be able to get out of bed that morning. *I need to enjoy the small things, to just live in the moment, and smile in the sunshine.*

"We're building a garden path," Robert said.

"You're what?"

"We're building a secret garden. We're starting with a stone pathway!" Robert shouted.

"Oh, okay, that's fine. You're welcome," Mrs. Van Kirk answered before giving them a smile and shuffling off.

I don't think she can hear a thing. We shouldn't have to worry about her.

They picked the third stepping stone to bury the pills under. They dug about three and a half feet down, wide enough to fit the rusty toolbox Robert had retrieved from the garage. Gordon put the pill bottles inside and then, after a quick glance around to make sure no one was watching, they buried the toolbox and affixed the stepping stone over it.

"All part of a good day's work," Robert said.

Gordon nodded as they slapped palms. He'd started the day feeling awful but now he felt much better.

27/ UNDER PRESSURE

Spring 1999

Your worst sin is that you have destroyed and betrayed yourself for nothing.

—Fyodor Dostoyevsky

Gordon fidgeted in his office chair as he waited for Robert and Todd. He felt the weight of his two worlds crushing down on him—a rising CEO of Sagan Software and a trending designer drug dealer. He gazed longingly at Bob Noyce on the wall. *I just wanted to be like you, Bob. I'm just not as sharp. Not as gifted as "Rapid Robert." I could have cleaned up my act and gone to MIT like you. I should have kept everything on the straight and narrow.*

Vikram leaned into Gordon's doorway, scowling. "The interns are being loud and unruly again. I cannot even concentrate on my work."

"Then tell them to quiet down. You're the Tech Lead. You have seniority, Vik. You outrank everyone at Sagan outside the executive leadership team," Gordon reminded him.

"Yes, but they don't listen to me."

Gordon stomped his foot on the floor and the noise settled down.

"They've also been playing inappropriate pranks," Vikram said.

"On you?"

"No, on Stuart. They took control over his computer screen and were opening explicit images."

"Let Robert and I worry about that. You stand up for yourself and we'll do the rest of the babysitting around here. I'll go downstairs to the basement intern pit after our leadership meeting and share a few words of warning."

Vikram looked unconvinced. "Okay."

Robert and Todd strolled into Gordon's office as Vikram left. "Come on in gents. Have a seat," Gordon said. "Todd, you're first. I want to hear about new business. How are sales?"

Todd grinned. "Chastain is working out well. I'm telling you guys, he's a closer. I know how to pick winners. We should all make a trip out to California for a meetup. Chastain is arranging something for us with a lead."

"Tell me more about that prospect."

"This isn't another service account—We're talking Silicon Valley, my homies. Startup money, Stanford grads. Silver spoons. They have a promising dot com startup idea; they just need a development team. And we get paid in equity too. Gordo, you've said it's all about getting ownership stakes early in a startup."

"But why would they go with Sagan Software for developers? Why source out of Nebraska? Surely they're connected with talented, high-caliber software developers all over the Valley."

"Because we cost less. A *lot* less. A certain breed of these young startups will be looking for lower cost development, and Gabriel Chastain knows where to find them. But it's not just a cost play, he's represented us as a boutique product development firm," Todd said.

"Get me a strawman proposal . . . include the monthly budget outlay. We need to control costs if this is a long-term investment," Gordon said.

Todd doodled on his yellow notepad, a satisfied smile on his face. He looked so smug with his frosted tips. Everything that he'd been tasked with so far, he'd delivered on. It was all working out for him, and Gordon couldn't help but hate him for it.

"I'd like a proposal with a budget," Gordon repeated. "Can you at least acknowledge me?"

Todd stopped doodling and slowly raised his gaze to meet Gordon's. "What's your problem, Gordon? I've always overseen P&L on my accounts. And I'm the CFO of Sagan Software!"

Gordon kicked his chair back and stood up from the table. "Fine Todd.

But how is there a P&L without any P?"

Todd threw his pen down and stood to face Gordon. "I'd say *I'm* the rockstar here—not you."

"This is my company, not yours," Gordon said, staring at him in disbelief. "So, get off your high horse!"

"It's *our* company, Gordon. How quickly you forget that I'm a co-founder!"

"Let's just calm down," Robert said. Gordon was shaking with anger, trying to hold himself back.

"You couldn't have done this without me," Todd said, taking a few steps closer to Gordon so he could tap him on the chest.

"Okay, sit down, please," Robert pleaded. "That's exciting news about California. I can go with you."

No one said anything for several seconds. If he backed down, Gordon knew Todd would, too. This wasn't how the meeting was supposed to go.

They both finally took their seats at the table. Gordon took a deep breath.

"And I need to talk with Barbara first if we're offering services for equity," he said, trying to get himself back on track. "If we're not even going to bill anything while staffing developers on payroll. And you can thank Barbara for the snacks in the breakroom, too."

"They're gross," Todd said.

"Anyways, let me know California trip details and we can arrange travel together."

"I'm heading out to California earlier," Todd said, without looking up from his notepad.

"Doesn't it make sense for us to all go out together?"

Todd continued to doodle, refusing to make eye contact. "I'll be making a stop on a break to visit some relatives out there. Isn't it a holiday week coming up or something? I think it might be good to have a little break from all this."

"Yeah, sure," Gordon said. "You do what you need to do."

But after the meeting was over and Robert and Todd left, Gordon replayed the whole interaction with Todd, his odd insistence that he head out there separately. He'd felt like something was up with Todd for a while now, though couldn't it just be his overall dislike for the guy? Compounded with all the rest of the stress he was dealing with?

You're just being paranoid. Everything's going to be fine. I just really loathe Todd.

{-----}

"Hello, good afternoon, Mr. Schroeder. I'm Senior Special Agent Parker and this is my partner, Special Agent Rasmussen. May we come in?"

Robert's heart jumped and his legs weakened as he stepped back to let the two agents in. He felt like he was going to pass out.

"Hi doggy. That's a nice doggy, there," Rasmussen said. "What's his name?"

"Uh, it's a girl. Her name is . . . uh, that's Betsie," Robert said, pained by the small talk.

"May we sit down?" Parker asked.

"Yes, please. What is this about? How can I help you two?" Robert was having a hard time controlling his breathing, too much or not enough.

"We'll get to the point, Robert," Parker said. "We're investigating a drug ring that we have evidence to believe is based in Lincoln. We know someone is selling MDMA, or a possible methamphetamine derivative, at parties in Nebraska, as well as distributing it outside of the community and across state lines. We have reason to believe that your friend and business partner, Gordon Hamilton, is involved somehow. We'd really appreciate your cooperation, Mr. Schroeder."

"Gordon?" Robert frowned. "That doesn't sound like him. We founded a tech startup together so we're always very busy. I'm not sure how he'd even have time for that. Gordon is an upstanding citizen, and gives back any time, all the time."

Rasmussen looked down at his clipboard. "We have just a couple quick questions today. Do you know anything about Gordon Hamilton's involvement in drug dealing in any capacity?"

"Gordon? Of course not."

"Do you know someone who goes by the name of Dino? It may be his street name."

"Dino? No, never heard of him. I think I would remember that name."

"Here's a card so you can call us any time." Parker handed Robert the card. "I trust you'll take the time to think about what you remember. Then do the right thing and tell us everything you know."

"I wish I could help, but I don't know anything." Robert thought about the pills buried in his backyard.

"We'll be back next week," Parker said.

"And then you'll have time to think about it and do the right thing. We can have a nice talk then," Rasmussen said.

"I'm sorry—that won't be possible. I'm going to California on a business trip next week."

"I would not recommend that you leave town any time soon. If you don't cause us trouble, we won't cause you trouble. It's as simple as that," Parker said. "We'll see you next week. Bye bye, doggy."

Robert closed the door firmly behind him and then leaned against the wall and felt his legs give way. His hands shook. Betsie came over and licked his face, trying to curl up in his lap. He patted her absently, his hands still shaking.

Gordon, what have you gotten yourself into?

{-----}

Gordon carefully drew the blinds in his office. He checked his speaker phone meticulously, then yanked it from the wall. He wadded it up and threw it in the storage closet for good measure. Gordon nodded conspicuously to his employees as he stormed through the cubicle farm, returning to his office with duct tape. He covered all the cracks in his door, window, and closet door with the duct tape.

Watch out for visitors too. And especially any electronic devices.

He had slept in late every morning of the week. He would dream peacefully and then wake up disturbed. He sat at his desk and reflected on his dreams, poignant yet fading, as if he was in purgatory.

His mind kept returning to Tonya. Her disinterest seemed clear enough yet he couldn't let go of the idea they just hadn't had the opportunity to really get to know each other, for things to click between them.

She doesn't seem to want to see me anymore unless she's using me for something. She's not interested in anything that I'm interested in.

Then, why do I like her at all? There must be something wrong with me.

Maybe I don't like her anymore.

Okay. Decided. Done.

If only it was that easy. Only in dreams.

He was jolted out of these thoughts by a knock at the door.

"Come in."

Vikram walked in and stood quietly, not his usual smiling self. He was too genuine for a good poker face.

"Can I shut the door?" Vikram asked.

"Yeah, sure. What's going on?"

"I don't even know how to start this conversation. We've worked together for a while, Gordon. Since FarmTrepid," Vikram said slowly. The moment he caught Gordon's eye, he looked away.

"Just say what is on your mind," Gordon said. "Please speak freely. This is a private conversation."

"Is something going on with you? Or Sagan? As in, between you and Todd, or Robert and Todd? It seems more dysfunctional here, like there is tension. Or division. Maybe I'm not describing it accurately. It's just . . . a feeling."

You're not the only one picking up on this.

"Conflict is part of running small startups, or any competitive business," Gordon said carefully.

"I know. And I'm glad I can talk to you about it. But Gordon, it seems more like chaos than conflict. I've loved this job, so it hurts me to say it. Almost as much as it hurts me to say . . . to say . . ."

"To say what?"

Finally, Vikram met his gaze. "I'm looking for another job. I wanted to be a part of something special. And I was, in a way. In other ways, I'm not really part of this. And I'm not having fun anymore."

"I appreciate you letting me know," Gordon said. "You'll certainly have my highest recommendation."

"Thanks," Vikram said uneasily. The sad expression on his face was only adding to Gordon's anxiety, but when Vikram left, Gordon felt relieved. He was glad Vikram would leave on good terms rather than follow them into the abyss.

{-----}

Gordon was the last person to join the phone bridge.

"Todd here. Robert is on as well," Todd said.

"Hi everyone. Okay, Todd, catch us up on Chastain," Gordon said.

"We had a great evening in San Jose. Chastain gave me a terrific summary of the opportunity and it's, like, as sweet as I had hoped." Todd spoke quickly, unable to contain the excitement in his voice. "We're proposing to own an entire development pod, from A-Z, project management, business requirements, development, testing, the whole enchilada."

"*We're* proposing? Who is we? Is that what the customer is asking for? Or is that just what Chastain is saying they want," Gordon said.

"Yeah. Well, dude, I haven't met them. But Chastain says it's like a bird, a blue bird," Todd said.

"A blue bird? What is that?" Robert asked.

"It's like a big opportunity that came from the sky and landed—like on your shoulder like a bird," Todd said.

Maybe Chastain was going to make it rain. But the sky was ominous.

"Like I said, Todd, I'm driving to California this week to join you," Gordon said. He wasn't that interested in hearing these blue bird metaphors. "We need to meet with the client and hear what they want. I want to hear it directly from them. Wait for me to arrive and arrange a meetup. Todd, schedule a briefing with Chastain and the meeting."

"When are you flying up, Rob?" Todd asked.

"I'm sorry, I'd love to join you, but I can't make it. I have a family emergency," Robert said.

"No biggie, homies. We're in good hands here," Todd said.

Gordon frowned. *Now Robert can't make it? What else can go wrong?*

He didn't say anything, though. He felt the walls closing in on him. He took several deep breaths.

I'm too deep into this. Past the point of no return. But I need a break or I'm going to have a meltdown.

A solo road trip across the country might do me good. Just the open road, music, sky roof, cigarettes, and my road atlas.

Go west, young man.

28/ RETURN FROM CALIFORNIA

Spring 1999

How could Y2K be a problem in a country where we have Intel and Microsoft.
—Al Gore

Gordon shoved a new CD in his stereo and set his cruise control. He was on his return home and had entered Nebraska territory from Wyoming— five hours more through the flat prairie. Gordon flew down the freeway, the windows down and sunroof open, air flowing freely, blowing away his distant problems. The timeless landscapes of the American West sprawled out as far as he could see. *The Oregon Trail, the real Old West. Where the buffalo roamed.*

After visiting cities in California and New York, Gordon felt like a changed man. Like the world was smaller. And he was a bigger part of it, more worldly, a fact he celebrated alone on the peaceful drive.

But as he approached the homestretch, worry crept into his mind as he thought back to that odd phone conversation with Robert. *And why hadn't he come to California? Something seemed off.* He decided his first stop once he got back into town would be to see if everything with Robert was really okay.

But not Todd, who cannot be trusted. Thank God he has nothing on me.

Just the Sagan business and his sales campaign. And the ethereal Chastain, more myth than man.

{-----}

Robert looked down at the toilet where he had flushed all the pills but one, which now sat on the palm of his hand. After inspecting the Y2K pill, Betsie followed him as he got a full glass of water to wash it down. It would take almost an hour to fully kick in, so sat on his sofa and watched the time anxiously.

He rubbed his arms and took a deep breath. *Relax.*

His heart pounded. Then it started to race. He stood up, overwhelmed, feeling first a tingling lightness that morphed into an overwhelming heaviness. He braced himself against the door jamb, shaking and sweating profusely.

He was not sure what he had done to himself.

Robert's vision blurred as he fought to keep up with the tidal waves rolling over him. He was lost in time and space. He let out a long gasp, traveling over a vast rainbow arc from relief to elation, to land on a fluffy cloud of pure bliss.

Betsie jumped on the sofa and licked his hand. The dog's tongue felt amazing on his hand, each sensation shooting up to his brain, saying *Hell Yes.* He massaged Betsie's furry back and rubbed his own hair and arms with pleasure.

Incredible.

Suddenly, Robert noticed daylight shining through a gap between the shades. Filled with paranoia, he jumped up from the sofa, stumbled across the room, and closed the shades. He turned off the lights, except for one dim lamp, and searched the drawers of the coffee table, then went to the kitchen, opening the drawers and pushing around the contents. He struggled to recall what he was looking for until he came across a lighter and realized that he had been looking for a cigarette all along. He found the pack sitting on the table. He was not going to risk going outside. Not to face the piercing daylight or the cutting cold gusts. Not to be crestfallen by the possibility of suspicious glances from neighbors.

He charged into the empty garage. He paced back and forth on the concrete in the dark. A rhythm was building up in his head, clenched jaw, and tightened fists. Right, the cigarette. He searched through his pockets until he found the pack of cigarettes. He frantically rummaged through front and back pockets again for the lighter. Paused, took a deep breath, and then realized the lighter was in the pack.

Flick, light, inhale, and a rush through his body. *Perfect.*

Robert went back inside to the bathroom and paused in front of the mirror. He recognized himself but at the same time it was not him. His eyes were completely dilated, big dark swelling balls of madness. He stared at individual goatee hairs. Took another deep breath and closed his eyes, trying to keep up with the rush. Then he moved in front of the toilet and lifted the lid. As he urinated, the toilet water swirled, and he felt closer and far away, like he had entered a Hitchcockian special effect. Robert felt no horror. On the contrary, he was thrilled by the dazzling effects, bubbles building, forming, and accumulating. The tingling stream went on and on. He lost track of time and the void seemed to go on for twenty or even thirty minutes. It was extremely satisfying. When he was finally done, he washed his hands, marveling at the sensation of the running water on his skin.

He finally made it back to the garage. His safe place. He pressed the headphones against his ears as the electronic tracks entered the second hour of continuous music. He lost track of time. The heavy beats lifted off as waves of flanger and EQ effects crashed over and reverberated. The interlude moment of respite tingled all over his head and arms. A new beat surreptitiously crept from the background and swelled. A tidal wave crashed with a crescendo into a new track, blooming into a metrical loop of vibrations that charged right through his body. Robert swayed his arms to the dark progressive house track. A syncopation of high percussion, synth, claps, hi hats, and a thumping bass drum, the music was more than just sound, it was something he could feel, fall into, completely lose himself in.

{-----}

And then a muddy, analog pounding noise broke through from reality. All at once, Robert's mountain peak fell into a deep valley, and with equal magnitude, his spirited highs switched to dreadful lows. Panic. Betsie barked and charged toward the front door.

Robert carefully opened the garage door leading into the house and closed it quietly behind him. He got down on all fours and crept toward the front of the house as Betsie continued to bark.

"Robert, if you're in there, it's me, Gordon. I'm back in town. So if you're at home, then let me in."

Robert crawled over, unlocked the deadbolt, and shuffled back toward the sofa. "You can come in."

Gordon entered the foyer. Betsie flip-flopped from guard dog to sellout ham, pawing at his legs, licking, wagging her tail.

"What in the hell are you doing, Rob?" Gordon asked. "Are you messed up or something?"

Robert managed to summon command of his body and staggered toward Gordon. He closed in on him, face to face, and pressed his index finger to his mouth tightly. Gordon was scowling but then nodded in agreement. Robert pointed all around the room to articulate his paranoia. He gestured to the garage.

Gordon followed him. "You are bugging out, man!"

Robert stopped straight, grabbed Gordon by the shoulders, and pulled him in.

"Yeah, I'm bugged," Robert whispered. "I'm bugged."

"Bugged?" Gordon mouthed the words.

"Bugged." Robert's face transformed, as if had had seen the depths of hell. "Busted."

He leaned his heavy forehead down on Gordon's shoulder.

"I'll take one of those cigarettes," Gordon said.

{-----}

Gordon managed to coax Robert into the living room. He was not comprehending what went wrong, recalling the good news he planned to share from the California trip. He was overloaded and reeling, trying to understand Robert's concern that the house was bugged. *But he's out of his mind and extremely paranoid.*

Then Gordon was struck by the realization of what Robert had really done. Robert had booked a round trip: the destination voyage was exciting, but the return trip was a lot weirder. He settled into his babysitting gig for the rest of the morning, marinating on everything that had happened in California. Chastain surprised them all with a great prospect but had not planned anything for the client meeting. Gordon wished Robert had been with them. Robert would have helped them improvise and contribute to technical discussion. Robert was always the most intelligent—just not today.

Robert mentioned something inexplicable about Gordon wearing an Indian chief headdress of feathers. He must be hallucinating. Gordon sighed. This was not the scenario he had envisioned coming back to.

{-----}

The two agents sat in an unmarked car only two houses down Robert's block. "What on earth are they doing in there? It sounds like they're doing drugs again. You'd think they'd have already learned their lesson," Parker said.

"Should we go in and give them a scare?" Rasmussen pushed back his wiry blond bangs, loosened his seatbelt, and dusted off a couple crumbs from his belly.

"No, just listen. Keep recording. They're going to talk about Y2K and incriminate themselves."

"You really think we'll be okay, Parker? I mean Y2K, the year 2000 glitch. I'm not a conspiracy theorist but I'll be stocking up on things like gasoline for my generator, bottled water, canned food, and guns."

Parker shook his head. "What, you think they're coming after your family? Like it's a zombie apocalypse or something?"

Parker pressed his earpiece. Rasmussen fidgeted in the glove compartment where he had stocked snacks for less cataclysmic outages.

"Why do we still care about Gordon anyway? We don't need anything else on Gordon. Robert has already given everything away," Rasmussen said.

"I want more. I want them to give up the identity of Brendan Carroll. Or, alternatively, we get so much evidence on Gordon, that he'll give up Brendan," Parker explained. "We don't know where Gordon Hamilton ranks in their power structure, but he may just be a mid-level player. We need to get a bigger fish. Our sources say that Brendan is the major connection to the organized MDMA trafficking cartel."

Rasmussen tore the plastic off another coffee cake. "Do we know whether Gordon even knows Brendan's real identity?"

"Now you're getting somewhere, young grasshopper. Now be quiet and keep listening to the tap."

Rasmussen made a face. "That music is so goddamn loud and repetitive. It sounds like a literal broken record. I can't even hear myself think while that crap is playing. Man, I hate that technological music. If you can even call that *music*."

"Hey, please don't take the Lord's name in vain," Parker said. "Not in my car, not on my case. But I'm with you one hundred percent—if you'll just cut out the blasphemy. I can't stand that techno music. It has no soul. There's not even lyrics to sing along with. They're not even playing any instruments. How can you enjoy music that isn't even performed by people playing live instruments?"

"Just a bunch of degenerate kids on drugs making noise with electronics. This country has lost its soul," Rasmussen said.

Parker sat up straight, pressed his earpiece. "Shh, shh, quiet. *Listen.*"

{-----}

Gordon searched Robert's cupboards and refrigerator for anything to eat. Betsie followed him like a shadow. He could make French toast with the rest of the bread, milk, and eggs. *Can syrup go bad? At least there's butter and cinnamon.* Betsie sat up and begged, paddling her front paws in the air.

"What did you say about bugs?" Gordon said as he cracked the eggs into a bowl.

"What? Drugs?" Robert asked.

"Turn the music down." Gordon walked over to the stereo to turn it down himself.

"Bugs, where? I don't see any?" Robert looked around at the walls and underneath the sofa and coffee table.

"Earlier after I got here, you said there were bugs," Gordon said.

Robert panted heavily, rubbed his head, and came down to earth for a moment of lucidity.

"The authorities are on to us. A special agent was here yesterday. We are being, uh, surveillance-d. They'll be on to you next."

"Why the fuck didn't you say something!?" Gordon shouted.

Robert jumped. "Don't scare me! I did tell you . . . didn't I?"

"I thought you were just being paranoid," Gordon said. "You're tripping man."

"I'm getting really freaked out I know I'm trippin' but you've gotta believe me." He and Betsie panted in unison. "I can't control my breathing or heart rate. Do you think I'm going to be okay?"

"*Agents* were here in your house!? What did you tell them? Did you say something about Dino? About Damian's source?"

"They already knew about Dino. They asked me about him," Robert said. "What do you even know about Damian's—"

"We should stop talking here," Gordon said.

"I'm having a bad trip. I need to lie down. Some place safe and warm." Gordon left a slice of bread soaking in the bowl of eggs and milk as he led Robert down to his bedroom and watched him climb into bed and pull the blankets over his head.

{-----}

Gordon headed straight for his office after the caretaking episode. Before he left, though, he had crept into the garage and inspected the evidence. He opened the door to the backyard and knelt to examine fresh dirt on the slab. Gordon followed the dirt back into the garage. The flood light had shined into the garage on a spade clumped with fresh soil. A smoking gun. And then that old toolbox on the workbench. Mystery solved.

Gordon's mind raced. *The toolbox was empty. What had Robert done with the rest of the supply? Maybe he had flushed the rest of it? If so, I would have found empty orange medicine bottles. Why didn't I look in the garbage can? I could go back and dig through the garbage before the agents do. No, I can't go back now.*

Gordon worked up a nervous sweat. He closed his office door for privacy. He needed to keep a low profile.

Robert had also mentioned that agents were at his house. Well, if he was talking any sense. What does that mean? Did he say he was bugged?

Gordon left his office to use the restroom, where he encountered his own reflection. The worst image he had seen all week. He recoiled from any deep reflection on what his friends and colleagues thought of him. *I'm a mess. Burning the candle from both ends.*

29/ DUST UP

Summer 1999

He says the best way out is always through.

—Robert Frost

At the house party, Robert's old roommate, Michael, now known as DJ Miracle Mike, was kicking out jams from two turntables. He had been booking more house parties lately and he pleased the crowd by playing old disco tracks to open the party, and then transitioned into house and techno late into the night.

Gordon had asked Robert to join him, but he was in no mood for a party. Not after the other wild night. *He's probably at home with Jennifer watching* Murder, She Wrote. Gordon cruised the house party, room to room, finding more crowds of insipid college students. He could not ever remember having too much fun at college house parties, but this was worse. It depressed him. It almost depressed him as much as the borderline humiliating message he'd left on Tonya's answering machine a few days ago. And she still hadn't returned his call.

Good riddance.

He returned to the dance floor to discover Oliver and Terrence dancing together, dressed like disco gods. Oliver wore a tight lime polyester leisure suit and pink wide-collar shirt. His shirt was unbuttoned and gawdy necklaces matted down in his sweaty chest hair. Terrence danced in only shiny tight shorts and a boa. Oliver waved and smiled. Terrence wrapped his boa around Gordon and pulled him against his bare chest.

"Um, thanks, I guess?" Gordon said to Terrence.

Terrence showed the conservative UNL students all his best disco dance moves.

Oliver knows how to be his true self. He always just wanted to be loved. He's not a hotshot like Todd but a good soul. He treats other people well.

"We're moving to San Francisco!" Oliver shouted over the music.

"I love San Francisco!" Gordon said. "And you'll love it there. But it's so expensive. Why would you want to move out there?"

"We're a young, mixed race gay couple. Do you think we'll just live out our days in rural Nebraska?"

Hell, half the people I know in Nebraska aren't even comfortable with straight men dancing. Not real men. Not even okay with just men dancing, not all the other gay stuff.

"So, you told your parents then? Are they taking it bad?" Gordon asked.

"Papa is uncomfortable. At least he's trying to accept it. My mom, she says she loves me for me. Maybe they've changed, maybe not. It's not them that we're worried about. It's everyone else, staring and judging all the time. It sucks to be stared at all the time," Oliver said plaintively.

Gordon had a puzzling sort of sympathy for Oliver. There was so much he did not know about Oliver. So many questions he had never asked, had never bothered to ask.

The house grew more packed with inebriated college students. Dance beats thumped and rattled. They shoved through drunk faces that Gordon found increasingly young and annoying. He and the odd couple, now in their early twenties, pursued better party venues.

{-----}

They followed Damian's directions out into the country, down gravel roads and a long driveway to an outdoor party. People socializing, drinking, and playing cornhole. Gordon and company found people in an open-door shed with mechanical tools, air compressors, and saws neatly organized, and a pool table on the slab.

Look, there's Dino at the pool table. Just like old times.

Gordon, Oliver, and Terrence attempted to join a conversation by a work-bench converted to a liquor bar. A big burly man was doing all the talking. He was broad and tall, ruddy tan skin, black leather vest, no sleeves, thick red hair in a wavy power mullet. His outsized beard gave the appearance of a lion's mane. His arms were thick barrels, not gym defined for looks, but for the strength to turn a wrench—or bend one.

The lion and his friends talked of hunting, rifles, handguns, and weapons that Gordon and his friends knew nothing about. And prime hunting spots for white-tailed deer. Gordon and his friends listened without speaking, like frightened little league outfielders praying the ball is not hit their way.

Dino walked by and shook Gordon's hand. "Hey Gordo, let's catch up later on." He locked eyes with the lion as if sensing another alpha male.

Dino patted Oliver on the shoulder and winked at Terrence as he made himself a vodka drink, teasing Oliver playfully before he lumbered back to the pool table.

"Hey youngblood, come over here. You know that tall guy?" the lion growled.

"Me?" Gordon asked.

"Yeah, I'm talking to you, champ. You know, the tall guy shooting pool with the rat tail on his chin. The one that just pinched your ass a minute ago. Don't bullshit me," the lion said, pointing at Oliver. Oliver turned crimson. The lion laughed.

"Dino?" Gordon asked, now facing the lion directly. He hated the way his voice came out high and squeaky.

"*Dino.* What kind of a name is that? You know that ain't his name! It's something else, just tell me his real name, youngblood," the lion roared.

"That's what I know him by. Dino. I swear."

"Well, know this. Your tall friend is a narc. Did your cupcake pal hear that too? He's a fucking narc," the lion said again, turning to Oliver.

Gordon shook his head, choked up and tongue-tied.

"Your friend is a fucking snitch," the lion's friend said, tapping Gordon's chest.

The lion and his pride strode out the open garage doors and across the yard to another group of burly mates. Terrence and Oliver whispered to each other.

"I don't feel good about it here, Oliver. We should leave," Terrence said.

"Let's just calm down. Dino is a badass. He can handle his business," Gordon said.

It must be that I've hit rock bottom and I've got nothing else to lose.

"I ain't playin'. Let's leave. Right now!" Terrence shouted.

"If Damian was here, you know what he would say. Just walk away. I know it," Oliver said to Gordon.

"Relax," Gordon said. "Let's make another round of drinks. It's a beautiful night. Look at this nice spread. Then we can pull Dino aside and see what's going on. Those guys are just flexing."

There must just be a rift or something between that burly guy and Dino. Show no fear. No fear.

Gordon and his friends hid behind the pool table while Dino finished his game. Dino stood waiting, towering over his cue stick, making it look small. He turned his back to measure up another shot.

The lion had come back in and chose that moment to charge Dino, his hungry pride not far behind.

A pool cue cracked loudly against Dino's neck. Arms and fists swung, beards flailed, leather jackets, dust, denim, all in a fury. Dino was knocked down on all fours, where he proceeded to get kicked and stomped with heavy boots. He covered his head but took many more shots to his body and ribcage.

Dino had somehow managed to break out of the dogpile and flee down the gravel driveway. The lion's pride gave chase into the darkness.

"I've got to go after Dino," Gordon said.

"We'll wait here for you." Terrence gave him a doubtful look. "Do you really think you should?"

"Be careful, Gordon. Don't get too close," Oliver said.

"They're gonna kill that poor guy. Should we call the police yet?" a female voice cried fearfully from beside the shed. A small crowd gathered and mumbled guardedly.

Gordon took off down the gravel driveway, the path barely visible in the dim moonlight. Just a flat gravel road with narrow shoulders. He slowed up his jog as soon as he was able to discern the hulking figures.

"If I were you, I wouldn't be bringing narcs around here no more," a figure shouted.

"Today is your lucky day, youngblood. We'll let you live this time. Someone vouched for you," the alpha lion growled.

Gordon walked into the ditch to pass safely around the departing pride. He jogged down the road toward Dino. The pitch of the sirens sharpened. Lights flashed on the road and pastures nearby.

"Are you okay?" Gordon asked, hunching down over Dino.

"Uhh. Ahhh. No," Dino moaned. "I think my ribs are broken."

Gordon looked around. "We've got to get out of here," he said. They wouldn't be sticking around to talk to the police.

30/ ALL THE KING'S HORSES

Summer 1999

All the King's horses
And all the King's men,
Couldn't put Humpty together again.

—Humpty Dumpty

Gordon drove westward as the Nebraska capitol building—known to locals as the "Penis of the Plains"—disappeared in his rearview. He pulled into a convenience store on the outskirts of town. The moody Nebraska weather switched from happy sunshine to brooding clouds. *It smells like it's going to rain.* The wind picked up.

Anyway, what do I care? I'm going to get busted. Robert meant what he said. There's a rat, Dino, or someone, I don't know. I'm not sure who to trust or who to turn to, but I'm not going back.

Not going back home.

I need to leave town.

Gordon dialed the squishy number pad on his cellular phone and extended the antennae for reception.

"I'm in a bit of trouble. I suppose I just needed someone to talk to," Gordon said.

"I'm sorry to hear that, Gordon. What can I do for you?" O'Neill asked.

Gordon listened to O'Neill's slow breathing. He didn't know how to start explaining. Not if his line was tapped.

"I took way too many risks, I don't know. I got greedy. Sorry, I can't say too much. It wouldn't be safe for either of us."

"Gordon, a wise man once told me that we don't all need to be millionaires. Not everyone can be in charge. Life isn't about putting everything into work. When you have kids, Gordon, you'll find out what life is all about."

"I appreciate the advice, really. I mean it. You know, I really miss Farm-Trepid. I wish I could go back there, just like the old days. Learning new things, working with friends. No stress of trying to spin too many plates. No fear of someone coming after you. If there was only a chance to start over and do it right."

"Are you in real trouble? Trouble with the law?"

"Yes, I think so."

"I'm sorry, Gordon. I'm terribly sorry to hear that."

"I wish I could go back and do it right."

"Life isn't like software. You can't undo mistakes in life."

"I know. I should have just . . . God, I don't know."

"Just do the right thing, Gordon. That's all I can tell you."

Gordon had one more call to make. And then he planned to dispose of his cellular phone.

"Hi Tonya, it's Gordon. Thanks for answering. How are you?"

"Gordon," Tonya said, sounding surprised. "Hi. I'm fine. What's going on?"

Gordon took a deep breath, his eyes fixed on the road in front of him. It all could have gone so differently. But it hadn't. With Tonya. With everything.

"I'm sorry if I seemed a little desperate or needy. I was just . . . hopeful, I guess. That something could work out between us."

There was a long pause. So long that Gordon wondered if Tonya had hung up.

"Gordon, I accept your apology," she finally said, sighing. "And it's nice that you called. But really, don't worry about me. Things are good and I haven't even thought about you, or us, at all. I mean, there was never really an *us*."

He couldn't help but smile, albeit sadly. "Well, you can't fault a guy for trying."

"And I don't, Gordon. And maybe I owe you an apology too—I should've been more upfront right away. I knew you liked me like that. And you're a great guy, Gordon, and you're really going to go places, I know it. It's just . . . we want different things from life. I just started seeing this guy and we really get along. He makes me feel good about who I am. We have a lot in common."

"I'm happy for you," Gordon said.

"You weren't happy with me before because you didn't like me for me. You had an idea of what you wanted and tried to fit me into it . . . before you even knew me for *me*," Tonya said.

It was true, he knew, but it still hurt to hear. "You're right," he said. "But, Tonya, can you just admit that you were leading me on? And that you were using me."

"If you admit that you were using me too. It's not like I understood what you wanted."

"You're right. That's also true."

"Remember when I told you that you were always chasing a dream? You were always searching for that pot of gold at the end of the rainbow. But, what's wrong with rainbows?" Tonya asked.

"And, what if there is no pot of gold?"

"I hope you find happiness, Gordon. I hope you find yourself somewhere out there, whatever you're chasing."

Tonya hung up. The rain pelted his car. Gordon's eyes welled with tears.

Why can't I accept myself? I could have been a good software developer. Good enough. I could have stayed on the straight and narrow in Nebraska all my life. Kept out of the fast lane. I could have had a little fun in college. Lots of people do. Stayed away from the criminal side. Away from drug dealing. Finished my degree.

I can't go back and change things. It will never, ever be the same.

Well, there's no life to return to now.

{-----}

"Where is Gordon today? We're supposed to meet with the interns this morning," Todd said to Robert.

"I don't know; he's not answering." Robert looked distracted and more stressed than usual. "I don't think Gordon's going to make it into the office today."

"Why do you say that?" Todd asked suspiciously.

"I don't know, he's not here yet, so I assume he's not going to make it. Let me go look outside." He walked out to the front porch, looked around the front and the back alley. Keeping an eye out for suspicious vehicles more so than looking for Gordon.

"Let's just go downstairs and address the interns together. We don't need Gordon," Todd said when Robert came back in.

The interns popped up across the cubicle farm like prairie dogs. Unlike Vikram, they had no hint of any issues with the Sagan Software leadership team.

"We're on track to close out an outstanding year at Sagan to bring in the new millennium. And for that, we want to share our gratitude, so we'll be throwing a summer party! We're having it professionally catered, so plenty of food and drinks to go around. Costumes are strongly encouraged, and prizes will be given out." Todd grinned.

"One last order of business, Todd. We'll be doing performance evaluations in the fall and each of you is up for a raise," Robert said. "And then—"

He was interrupted by Todd's phone.

"Excuse me," Todd said. "I've got to get this."

He walked up the stairs and into the backyard.

"It's Hank. What's happening there?"

"Well, is it all sorted out?" Todd asked.

"Yes, but there's one last piece of the puzzle. I need you and your dad to help me get in front of Gary. You'll have to protect us from the Sagan side of things. Just let me talk to your father about the part with Gary," Hank said.

"Gary is a nutjob. But he's a genius too."

"I have a way with folks like that." Hank didn't sound concerned. "Listen, Arthur has already started a buzz in New York before we officially get Gary to sign. He says he has prospective buyers. Deep, deep pockets. Arthur will create a bidding war. These buyers want all of Gary's business, product & IP, and subscribers. Arthur loves the multi-level marketing aspect too. So, we're going to wrap it up with a bow on top. Can you believe that?"

"I believe it. Arthur has the Midas touch," Todd said.

"He's a raider, that Arthur Ravencrow. So, Frank was quoting scripture again. And Arthur told Frank that anyone saying the meek shall inherit the earth is probably taking you for a ride. I think it offended Frank. He's like religious or LDS or something. He's a damn good lawyer is what he is," Hank said.

"Too funny," Todd said stiffly.

"I told you about that time in college when Arthur and I went out on a boat at the—"

"Shit, Robert's coming looking for me. I was just in the middle of talking to the interns about an office party," Todd said.

"Go attend to your business. For now, anyway. I'll get in touch with your father. Catch you later," Hank said.

Todd hung up and tried to wipe the look of guilt off his face before Robert reached him.

{-----}

"No, not everything is lost." Barbara forced a smile, hoping it conveyed confidence and reassurance to her husband, who had a horrified look on his face. "Just the savings. And 401k retirement. We still have our nest egg, those precious Beanie Babies."

"Are you saying all our retirement and savings are gone? What about the disabilities we saved?" Henry asked, choking up.

"You'd been out of work so long, Henry. It's been all on my shoulders. Just me." Barbara's smile faltered and she broke down. The dining room table wobbled against her frame.

"Can we get more from the computer company boys?" Henry asked frantically. "The Sagans? They're flush, aren't they?"

"I don't know. I don't know. It's not right," Barbara said.

"But can't they afford it? Didn't you say they were the bad guys?" Henry said.

"Yes, I think so."

"We're good people. We're good Christian people."

"Yes, you're right we are."

"And then when do we stop? How much is left?"

"Not much," Barbara sobbed.

Henry dabbed his eyes with his handkerchief.

"You haven't had a bite all day. What do you want for dinner? I can put some pot pies in the stove," Barbara said, wiping her eyes.

"I reckon nothing. I'm not hungry no more."

"Did you feed the cats?"

"Not yet," Henry said, sighing. "I'm just goanna watch *Rikki Lake.*"

He cleared a place on the couch to sit, a moaning cat clinging to the middle cushion.

Knock, knock.

Hard raps on the front door.

"*This is the police! Open the door. We have a warrant for your arrest!*" an unfamiliar voice shouted.

Barbara jumped from the table and ran for her office like a blitzing defensive tackle. She yanked a stack of papers out of a cabinet, flung them in the bathtub, and turned on the hot water.

"*Come out with your hands up so we can see them! We have a SWAT team out here. We're knocking down the door if you don't open.*"

Barbara reversed past Henry as she swept back through the kitchen and out the sliding back door.

"Hurry up, Henry!" she hissed.

"But my—"

"Just run, Henry! They're gonna know your back injury is bunch of horseshit!"

"But—"

"You go first, hurry it up!" Barbara shouted.

Henry ran through the backyard and deftly climbed over the chain link fence. He escaped into the narrow path between the backyard fences and into the brush.

Then Henry galloped out of view like a three-year-old stallion.

Barbara charged for the back fence with all her momentum and threw herself against the chain link, nearly knocking it over. The fence rebounded and flipped her on her back. She struggled to get to her feet, a sharp pain in her lower back, as she started the climb by squeezing her hands and feet between the steel wires. She somehow managed to flop herself half over the top rail and became hopelessly stuck. She grunted, shook, and squealed, "Henry! Save yourself!"

"I can't believe it. The big one is trying to make a run for it. Get her!"

The two armored men from the SWAT team took off across the lawn. They ripped Barbara off the fence, shredding her house dress. The SWAT team sergeant pressed Barbara's face down in the wet grass and hand-cuffed her.

"Where'd the little man go?" crackled over the headset.

"The little bastard is quick. Who said that he was disabled?!" the sergeant said.

"He's heading down the back alley. We're in pursuit. Send backup, he could be armed!" the headset blasted.

"Copy that. Officer, go, go! Send the K-9. Female suspect is in custody. Repeat, we have caught the white whale," the sergeant said to his headset.

"Bahaha, I can't breathe! Bahaha. Why'd you throw me down?" Barbara cried.

"Why'd you run? Did you think you were going to get away?" the sergeant asked.

"I didn't do anything, asshole," Barbara grunted.

"Then why'd you run? It's funny, lady. I do this a lot. And it always surprises me how all the innocent ones run. Strange, isn't it?" the sergeant said.

"I'm innocent. What is this about?" Barbara cried. "Get off me!"

"He's fast but we got him, thanks to our K-9 friend. He suffered a pretty nasty bite on the buttock," chirped the headset.

"Settle down," the sergeant said. "Get up, lady. We're taking you and your husband downtown."

The sergeant leaned down to help Barbara up but fell forward to the ground, unable to lift her bulk.

"I'm gonna need backup here," the sergeant said in his headset.

On the top of the fence, a shred of flower-patterned fabric flapped in the wind.

31/ THE CLUBS

Summer 1999

No one can earn a million dollars honestly.

—William Jennings Bryan

"Oh, shit, Hank. You sliced it again. I think it's that grip. Here, you can use my clubs," Denny said.

"I don't think it's the clubs, Denny," Hank said. "I'm not much of a golfer."

"And Frank was just following us around with that cart. Where did he go? Anyway. Let's take a break. Another Arnold Palmer?"

"Oh, I think it's time for a gin and tonic," Denny said.

Denny and Hank refreshed beverages off the teeing ground at the Oak Hills Country Club.

"Okay, buddy, I need you to vouch for us with Gary," Hank said. "We're going to do a complete buyout, but we need to keep him around at least six months past the transition. He's essential. I know you and Gary are close, from church or whatever, but we're like brothers, Denny."

"Frat brothers," Denny said.

"You're damn right, buddy." Hank lifted his glass as if he were offering a toast. "Let me talk to Gary about an acquisition. Arthur Ravencrow will fix it all up. The Corinthian legal team is getting Frank prepared with some preliminary reviews, we just need get it in front of Gary and get him to sign on the dotted line. I'll get you a piece of the pie."

"All I need is a finder's fee, Hank. It's a shame I was so much older than you in college. The three of us would have had a hoot," Denny said.

"Denny, the stories we would have made. Arthur was always the brilliant prodigy. Fraternity president, athlete, scholar, but oh, God was he ever wild in college." Hank grinned and shook his head at the memories.

"I'm surprised he graduated with a clean record. I suppose streaking isn't a felony," Denny mused.

"You know Arthur now—all buttoned up—he'll know what he's doing."

"But what about Sagan Software?" Denny asked in a more somber tone. "Didn't they have a deal for part ownership?"

"Nothing was ever put into writing and signed. Sagan Software are amateurs. It was just a verbal arrangement between Gary and a consulting service provider. We'll need Todd to smooth things over," Hank said. "He's done a great job so far."

"I'll make it happen. I'll appreciate the finder's fee. But I still don't get it, Hank. What is the long play?"

"Gary's a mad genius. He's bottled lightning. And it may not even be that long of a play for Arthur. He thinks he'll find a buyer quickly, especially with the backing of his partners and their deep connections in the finance industry. Surely, you've heard Gary's vision about electronic trading and everything behind that."

"Ha, Gary's said a lot of things. I'll make it happen. I'll try to make sure it's when Gordon isn't around," Denny said.

Hank shook his head vehemently. "Gordon can't be there! Listen to me. I'm serious. He can't even know. Robert can't know either, cause he's in cahoots with Gordon. Todd needs to know how to keep a secret. Or else."

"How long have you been cooking up this scheme?" Denny asked.

"Too long," Hank exclaimed. "Before they even met Arthur Ravencrow in New York. What, you think I just wanted to help Gordon? Just mentor some young guys so I can feel good about myself?" He chuckled. "That's quaint, Denny."

"You're ruthless, Hank. But yeah. I'll talk to Gary. Gordon won't know."

"Oh, here comes, Frank. What a snooze. Fun's over."

"He can take us back to the clubhouse to get a real drink."

{-----}

"Ice cream?" Parker could barely hide his look of disgust. "A dadgum ice cream trip does not trump the Y2K case, Raz."

"Just cuss once for me, Parker," Rasmussen said.

"How's Todd coming along?" Parker asked.

"He's a godsend. He wants to walk away clean, so he'll give us anything about Sagan Software business and finances. It's Gordon and his associates. Not Todd and Sagan Software. Todd never knew. Zero evidence to involve him. And Robert will be off the hook as soon as he flips. We'll wire him up too," Rasmussen said.

"And the latest on Barbara?"

"After we reported her to the FBI, they sent in a police SWAT team and brought her in. Good old Barbara and her husband were running a nice little racket there. Embezzlement and fraud. Made off with some of the dirty drug dealing money and cooked the Sagan books. And selling counterfeit Beanie Babies and moving them across state lines."

"That's terrific, Raz. I'm doubtful Barbara was directly involved in the drug business. We have no evidence of that. She was probably aware that Sagan's cashflow was nefarious and took advantage of it for her own benefit."

"Yes, but she was a risk all along. Not to be trusted."

"That's why large companies do background checks. An employee like Barbara who is in debt or somehow financially compromised is a company risk."

"Yeah. Exactly. And don't fall for that 'Hello, honey' talk from her. That woman is diabolical."

"She's a wolf in. . . ."

"Rosanne's?"

". . . clothing."

"You complete me."

"Cut it out, Raz."

{-----}

Gary's wife led Denny, Todd, Hank, and Frank into the dining room. "He's all yours," she said. "You can have him."

"Aren't I popular lately," Gary said. "My dance card is filling up."

Denny smiled. "As Todd probably explained, we're working with a VC in New York that is interested in acquiring your company."

"Is this the same kind of offer as Sagan?"

"No. Let's be clear." Denny coughed. "We're not representing Sagan in any way. This would be a full acquisition from a separate and new entity. They may or may not choose to solicit Sagan's service. Let me introduce you to Hank, who is our conduit, and his lawyer, Frank."

"As I already told Todd and Gordon, I'm now ready to sell out and move on. This sounds lucrative. Where is Gordon anyway? Shouldn't he be here? He hasn't returned my call today either," Gary said.

"Gordon is traveling. Even a CEO needs a breather. Besides, he trusts Todd. Wasn't it Todd and I that made the connection in the first place, Gary?"

"Hmm, okay." Gary frowned. "I just need you all to get on the same page. I had a strange call a couple weeks ago from Barbara, the Sagan accountant. She was requesting a direct cash payment. Gordon usually does a pickup but maybe he's too busy. How does Barbara not know that Sagan was working for equity and the billing arrangement has changed?"

"Might just be a communication issue, Gary. Small companies and everything," Denny said. "Again, I would take that discussion offline with Sagan."

"For the record, we're a separate entity. Sagan's business is none of ours," Frank said.

"Just set it straight with Barbara, Todd. Anyway, what do you need from me next?" Gary asked.

"Frank and I are going to set up a time to review your finances, subscriber list, renewals, and software assets," Hank said. "Then Frank will have you go over some preliminary paperwork. Legal stuff. It's all straightforward."

"Robert was instrumental in the new web application design, but he didn't do much implementation. Have you talked to Stuart yet? Let's bring him in when we review the software. Honestly, I didn't like him at first either, but he's done a big share of the programming," Gary said.

Denny looked at Todd. "Do you think Stuart is a key player? Should we work out some sort of retainer?"

"Stuart Sandberg? No way, Dad. He's replaceable. He'll be chasing volcanoes," Todd said.

"Oh, right, he's that strangely dressed kid you had over with all the food allergies."

Gary tossed a rubber basketball up in the air. "So, I'm a little confused. Is Frank with the New York outfit?"

"Frank is my attorney and partner, out of Omaha," Hank said. "We'll be assisting Corinthian Ventures, the VC out of New York City. I'm sure they'll have their own M&A lawyers, but we're responsible with the due diligence and preparation."

"Thank goodness. I was tip-toeing around like you were from Corinthian. So, you aren't a couple elitist New York City liberals?" Gary said.

"Oh Lord no. I'm as conservative as they come," Hank said, laughing, "We're from Omaha, Gary. I went to college with Denny. Go Big Red!"

"New York City—it's like a den of thieves. They're trying to suck the soul out of the heartland red states, or what those assholes call the flyover states. Please pardon my French. I rarely swear. They're elitist, socialist hypocrites."

Hank grinned. "I'm a card-carrying capitalist, Gary. Keep the government out of my business, protect the second amendment, end all entitlement programs, freedom from—"

"Amen. Have you read Ayn Rand?" Gary asked.

"*The Fountainhead.* Howard Roark, and the—"

"A man after my own heart. Finally, talking to someone with brains and a soul. Listen, since we're all friends here, you need to be getting ready for the year 2000 problem. Y2K is going to wreak havoc," Gary said.

"What are you thinking, Gary?" Frank perked up after sitting quietly for so long.

"Catastrophic, Frank. Power grid outages, industrial control system failures, a run on the banks. But I'll be ready. I'll have my bunker completed by the fall. But not like I'm going to let you guys in on it—I haven't even told my wife."

"That is a prudent plan. How long do you think you can last down there?" Frank asked.

"Nuclear fallout notwithstanding, I can probably live down there for three years or so."

"I have a good VHS tape you can borrow from Reverend Jimmy Powell. I ordered it through the mail from a 1-800 number. Very informative, and from a biblical perspective," Frank said.

"Make me a copy, Frank. Come on back to my office guys, I have a few more things to tell you about," Gary said.

32/ COLUMBUS CIRCLE
Fall 1999

The year 1999, seventh month,
From the sky will come a great King of Terror
—Nostradamus

Todd and his father, along with Arthur, Hank, and Frank sipped expensive cocktails at an upscale Manhattan bar. Todd stepped away from their conversation and sidled over to the Steinway & Sons grand piano. He gazed at the Columbus Circle beneath him. In the roundabout, yellow cabs endlessly followed yellow cabs. The foliage of Central Park was fading into the chartreuse, gold, and auburn of autumn.

"Todd, cheer up," Arthur said when Todd made his way back over. "What else could you possibly want?"

"I want you to order the most expensive scotch on the menu," Denny said.

"Life lesson. Don't spend what you haven't earned, young man." Hank looked at Arthur.

"Are you sure that it's going to close?"

"Yes, well, I'm ninety-nine percent sure. The deal is signed and fully executed; closing date is planned. There's almost zero concern from the regulators."

"How much again? I can't count that high," Hank said.

"One hundred seventy-three million dollars," Arthur said coolly.

Hank let out a low whistle. "We're making Gary Stanley a millionaire too. He still held a minority share, like nearly fifteen percent."

"Fourteen and a half percent," Frank said.

"All is fair in mergers and acquisitions," Arthur said.

Hank raised his glass.

"To Arthur Ravencrow, the architect! The mastermind! And to Todd, the lead generator!" He was about to take a sip but stopped and looked at Denny. "And Denny for creating Todd!"

"Please, please. Gentlemen, the pleasure is all mine," Arthur said, "Anyway. One of my partners at Corinthian laughed when I told him I had a venture way out west in Nebraska—"

"Laughing all the way to the bank now. Corithian cleaned up too."

"Cheers to Hank Sherman for explaining everything, and helping me wrangle Gary along," Denny said. "To Gary, may he outlive us all after the mayhem of Y2K, safe and alone in his bunker."

"What about that drug dealing nonsense?" Arthur said. "Should we worry? Frank, tell us again, please. Tell us we're clean so we can enjoy another round."

"Gary's enterprise was a separate entity altogether," Frank said. "Sagan Software was just a service provider. The only contracts executed between Sagan and Gary were a Master Service Agreement, NDA, and just some simple invoices and change orders for services rendered. The equity agreements were verbal only. And there were conflicting sides to that agreement. Nothing is legally binding. Sagan Software will go into administration. I don't see it surviving, especially with Gordon Hamilton on the run and Robert being questioned. I've recommended legal representation for Todd, but he's clean."

"Enough serious talk. I've got a joke. How are software salesmen different from used car salesmen?" Hank said.

"Go on," Denny said.

"Used car salesmen know when they are lying," Hank said.

"Okay, here's a good one. There are only two industries that call their customers users: illegal drugs and software," Arthur said.

"Oh, that's good," Hank said. "So, here's whole the story from the beginning, gentlemen. Todd turned me on to them, and they proposed that first deal for the boating site, but that fell through. And then—"

Frank groaned. "No more stories, Hank, please."

"Okay, okay, fine," Hank said. He turned to Todd. "Why don't you share the story you told me earlier?"

Todd frowned, wishing he could be anywhere else but where he was. It was supposed to be a celebration, but he felt miserable.

"No, I'm not telling them, Hank. Not now," Todd said. He pulled his shirtsleeves out from under his suit jacket.

Hank waved him off. "Okay, fine. I'll tell it then. So, Robert," Hank said, waving his cocktail-laden hand as he spoke. "You know, his other partner, at Sagan—"

"Robert was the CTO of Sagan Software," Todd interjected.

"Right. So, Robert knew about the drug dealing or whatever. From Gordon. They were close friends. But Robert wasn't part of the nefarious business. He was getting pressured by the DEA or whoever. But he figured it was Damian, you know, the drug weirdo. Robert told them about Debbie and that she was pregnant with Damian's child."

"You're telling it all wrong, Hank," Todd said. "Damian and Debbie were together, that's no secret. The pregnancy was a secret."

"See Todd, this is why *you* should have told the story."

"So, did Robert give them up? I still don't understand the issue. You're a terrible storyteller, Hank," Arthur said.

"Yeah, why does it matter, Hank?" Frank asked.

"Robert didn't give anything up," Todd said. "He never snitched or betrayed his friends." He paused. "It was me. I told them about the books. About everything I knew. I told everyone about Debbie's pregnancy. They knew it was Damian's child and they exposed that weakness. And the worst part is it will come back on Robert and not me." He stared at a droplet of water on the table. When he raised his head, his father was looking at him closely.

"I helped the DEA, and I helped you all, but I, I—" Todd said, growing more and more upset.

"Ah, now it makes more sense," Hank said. He looked around the table. "How can anyone expect me to tell a good story if I don't have all the facts? And anyway, good on you, Todd. You're a millionaire now."

Millionaire or not, Todd couldn't sit there and listen to this any longer. He got up and stormed off, ignoring everyone's calls to return.

{-----}

"So, here's the latest update on Brendan Carroll, aka Dino," Rasmussen said. "I talked to him at the hospital. He's going to cooperate. He was never a big-time mover and shaker. Just another middleman, trying to make it big. He's in bad shape but he'll pull through. He asked to join the witness protection program, change his identity."

Parker snorted. "Who does he think he is? Henry Hill? He's watched way too many movies."

"Are we going to celebrate or what?" Rasmussen asked.

"Sure, I'll take you out for dinner. We can go to the Carlos O'Kelly's. It's about time you got a real meal instead of all that junk food."

"And drinks?"

"Drink on your own time," Parker replied sternly. "Fine. I'll let you order one margarita."

Raindrops struck the windshield like heavy pellets.

"It's cats and dogs out here. Nebraska weather. Did we get the results from the lab on Y2K?" Rasmussen asked.

"No. Not yet," Parker said.

"Friendly wager?"

"That's beneath me. No betting."

"What? C'mon. After a job well done," Rasmussen said.

"Okay, fine. I'll guess. I think it's a cocktail. Just a mixture of ecstasy and some other stuff. Could be meth and cough syrup. Nothing new, none of this designer drug nonsense."

"So, you don't believe what Damian's saying?"

"What, that he claims to be an alchemist or other drug-fueled nonsense."

"No, that he got a confidential and proprietary formula developed by a European pharmaceutical company. That there was a leak. He had met a lab scientist through chemistry clubs at the university. He obtained the formula and ingredients from an insider." Rasmussen shrugged. "Could be something to it."

"So, Y2K was a drug designed by a European pharmaceutical company through an R&D project?" Parker asked incredulously.

"Well, it's possible."

"It could be a diversion. It's far-fetched."

"But is it? Parker, we know where many of the popular recreational drugs came from. LSD was created by a Swiss chemical company. Ecstasy was synthesized by Merck pharmaceutical in Germany. And who isolated cocaine? Take a guess, Parker," Rasmussen said.

"Bayer?" Parker guessed.

"Close. Another German chemist. Stranger than fiction, and don't get me started on methamphetamines during World War II—"

"But, back to Brendan Carroll. He's supposed to get released from the hospital today."

"Then let's go pick him up."

"And then Gordon Hamilton?"

"All in good time, Special Agent," Parker said. "Brendan Carroll first. He'll pour his heart out. Then we'll go find Gordon Hamilton, armed with some damning information."

"We still haven't found a lab," Rasmussen said.

"No labs yet. Maybe your European pharma theory holds water."

{-----}

Gary and the construction superintendent stood over the workbench in the dusty jobsite trailer.

"This is the kitchenette here and dining room," the superintendent said, sliding his finger over the blueprints. "Let's go outside. I'll show you where the entryway will be."

"And they'll bring in trees to cover this area from the street?" Gary asked.

"Of course, let me show you. It should hide everything from the highway. And the gravel path will be discreet. You'll have the CCTV cameras over here—" the superintendent pointed— "and there."

A backhoe rumbled, puffed out black smoke, and clawed into the hard Nebraska dirt.

"I need all workers to sign the privacy and non-disclosure agreements. I'll need those as soon as possible," Gary said.

"Of course, Gary. You'd be surprised how many of these underground shelters I'm doing. Y2K has been a boon for us."

"Don't get me started," Gary said.

"And thank you for your referral to Frank." The superintendent paused.

"But this is the Taj Mahal of bunkers. The indoor basketball hoop will be one of a kind. Can I ask—what do you do for a living?"

Gary laughed. "You can ask."

"Probably computer stuff."

33/ WESTBOUND ON I-80
Fall 1999

You can't get away from yourself by moving from one place to another.
—Ernest Hemingway

Gordon barreled down I-80, the Gateway to the West, through central Nebraska following the Platte rivers. In the 1800s, this was the real Old West, yonder from Buffalo Bill Cody's ranch, a high plains crossroads for cattle trails. Then the frugal Nebraskans paved I-80 through the cheapest path and least scenic path, the totally flat Platte River flood plain. *All the romance of western movies is long gone. Just boring land to be derided by people from California to New York.*

Gordon consulted his trusty and weather-worn atlas. He could go south toward Denver through Albuquerque to El Paso and hop the border to Mexico and keep heading south. Or head north toward Montana and into the wilderness, perhaps across the Canadian border.

Keep going west. Westward ho.

White fence posts and telephone poles whirled by in a blur.

If I had just accepted my lot in life. If I didn't have my head in the clouds, would I be here now?

No, it was Todd. Todd was the problem. It was always Todd. Don't trust anyone, especially not a weasel like Todd.

Damian Charlock, the alchemist. He pulled me to the dark side. That guy was never in touch.

Why didn't Robert try to stop me? Oh, but he did warn me. He tried to help, and I didn't listen. Robert was looking out for me. Such a good friend and I screwed things up for him too.

Welcome to Wyoming. Forever West.

Pine Bluff.

Was it all worth it? Did I achieve my dreams?

Springing from the flat, colorless plains stood a white statue of Madonna. Over thirty-feet tall. Gordon turned the car into the drive—a rutty, unpaved road—to make an unplanned pilgrimage. The sign read, "Welcome to Our Lady of Peace Shrine."

With software, we can roll back our changes. But not in life. Some things can't be undone.

He parked the hatchback and got out. He looked up at the statue, lit a cigarette, inhaled, reflected.

When will I find peace with myself.

Hail Mary! Let me find peace.

{-----}

Gordon checked into the cheap motel frequented by roadrunners and tumbleweed. He told the innkeeper, a kind, middle-aged Chinese man, that he would pay in cash. He was a long way from that dorm room where he and his roommate had hung movie posters.

He walked across the scrubby parking lot, tall weeds breaking through the pavement, an old rusty shopping cart on its side. He took his bag and atlas from the car and threw them on the creaky bed. It was quiet. He was alone. The front door opened to the parking lot, the desert, the mountains, the Pacific, the end of the world. Beyond the back wall of this motel was nothing. Nothing.

He decided he was going to find the end of the world. He imagined bribing his way onto a cargo ship to South America, to the Pacific, and beyond. He brought enough money to pay his way around the world. More cash than he should ever need.

Quoth the Ravencrow: "Cash is King."

He woke early in the morning without any alarm. It took him a few moments to remember where he was. He stood by his car in the parking lot, the sun blazing on his neck, pleasantly warm for that time of year. His trusty road atlas had faded and fallen apart; the cover torn off. He had found solitude.

Let me drive away in peace.

{-----}

The innkeeper hung a plastic room key on a hook in the back office. Another long shift. The deadbeat assistant had called in sick, so he said. His wife could not cover for him either. She was taking care of the children that he sacrificed so much of his life for. It was going to be another long night.

The door swung open. Two men wearing black jackets approached the counter.

"May we speak to the manager of the motel?"

"Yes, I'm the manager."

"I'm Senior Special Agent Parker and this is Special Agent Rasmussen. We're with the Drug Enforcement Agency. We have reason to believe that a suspect on the run may be coming through this area."

"I see," the innkeeper said. "How can I help you?"

"We have a few photographs. We'd like you to look at them and let us know if you might have seen the suspect in the area," Rasmussen said.

The innkeeper had dealt with the police before. In his thirty-plus years at this motel, he had seen his share of crime scenes, occasionally bloody and violent. But he'd never had the DEA show up.

"Come back to my office, follow me," he said to the two agents. "Please have a seat."

"Have a look at these pictures . . . And these as well." Rasmussen placed several photos on the innkeeper's desk. In a large, color photograph, a young man posed on the high school steps in a letter jacket and baggy jean shorts.

"Yes, I've seen him. He left yesterday morning. He was quiet, didn't cause any trouble, traveling by himself—"

"Do you know which way he was heading?" Parker asked.

"Oh, I wouldn't know that. He left the key here at the front desk. Then he was gone."

"You've been very helpful, sir," Rasmussen said.

"I can show you the room if—"

"No thank you, sir. Raz, come on, let's go!" Parker said.

They peeled out of the parking lot, tires squealing.

"Perps typically go somewhere they know. He's heading toward the West Coast. California. He knows the Bay Area. According to his friends, he's taken this route before, too," Parker said.

"The motel said he's paying in cash. We never found his money stash. He must be flushed with cash. I can't even imagine how much." Rasmussen shook his head. "And can you believe we got nothing out of Robert? He knows we've been recording him. He must know more."

"He does," Parker said with certainty. "We have a good case to charge him with obstruction of justice."

"He probably thinks he's being a good friend. Not ratting out Gordon."

Parker smirked. "We'll see if he perjures himself. This isn't over for him yet, either."

"True friendship is a rare thing," Rasmussen said, staring out at the remoteness of Nevada's outback.

{-----}

Gordon climbed over a hill to see what was on the other side. Nothing but rugged desert covered with yucca and sagebrush. He imagined hiking into the desert and disappearing, only to be found by vultures, the arid desert and the sands of time taking all but a half-buried skeleton.

The isolation triggered an empty yearning. He tried to remind himself of all the good times. How the wild parties and drugs had made him feel. The best feeling of his life. He attempted to revel in those memories but there was nothing but emptiness.

Emptiness and the certainty that he would miss his friends deeply, the fun times they had, the way things could have gone if only he had made different choices.

He scrambled down the hill to the flat desert and jumped back into his car. He opened his sunroof, rolled down the windows, and turned the music up.

California, here I come. And then to the end of the world.

{Acknowledgements}

This book would not have happened without my editor Erica Smith, who stuck with me through it all—from beta reading, developmental editing to the final copywrite phase. Again, Ashley outdid herself with the cover design and book formatting. I was so pleased with *Simon versus Simon*, but this design is even better.

I want to thank everyone, especially friends and family, who have supported my writing. For supporting *Simon versus Simon* and telling me not to give up on this Y2K manuscript. My love and gratitude for my wife Melissa, who encouraged me to keep going.

And special thanks to Matt Keller for last-minute feedback from a real DEA agent.

My pets, the cause of many typos and distractions, but the greatest companions.

In Memory of Bentley, 2006–2021